EMERALDSEA

SUNRISE

John
Enjoy!

Richard Grant

**WORKS BY
RICHARD LEWIS GRANT**

The "I LOVE TO READ" Series:
SILVERGLADE ~ THE DREAM
SILVERGLADE ~ PEOPLE OF LIGHT
GOLDENROD ~ SECRET HOPE
GOLDENROD ~ MYSTERY
GOLDENROD ~ DARK OF NIGHT
EMERALDSEA ~ NIGHTMARE
EMERALDSEA ~ SUNRISE

APS HOMESCHOOL SURVIVAL GUIDE

THE READING GATE

EMERALDSEA
SUNRISE

CƷ

Richard Lewis Grant

APS Publishing
A division of
Advantage Preparatory Schools, Inc.

Published by APS Publishing®
A division of Advantage Preparatory Schools, Inc.
PO Box 802274
Santa Clarita, CA 91390
APS@TheVine.net
www.GreatBooks4me.com
www.facebook.com/RichardLewisGrant

This is a work of fiction. Names, characters, places and incidents
are products of the author's imagination. Any resemblance to
any actual person, living or dead, events, or locales is entirely
coincidental.

Cover photo: Ryan and Brittany Secor
Cover design: Daniel Moyer and R. L. Grant
Photo of author: Donna Henri

Printed in the United States of America

ISBN-13 978-1500300661
ISBN-10 1500300667

Dedication

To
Brittany Nicole (Grant) Secor
and her husband Ryan Lee Secor

I've not lost a daughter, I've gained a son.

With all my love,
Richard Lewis Grant

Acknowledgments

I had hoped I could complete this book in time for Brittany and Ryan's wedding, but wedding plans proceed much faster than books. So now, it comes a little after their 1st anniversary. Mazel tov!

Telling bedtime stories is one thing, making them into books is quite another. Many hands and hearts have helped turn the original "Adventures of Quasar and Nemo" into "Silverglade: The Dream", "Silverglade: The People of Light", "Goldenrod: Secret Hope", "Goldenrod: Mystery", "Goldenrod: Dark Of Night", Emeraldsea: Nightmare and now "Emeraldsea: Sunrise".

Though a complete list would be much longer, I would especially like to thank:

Cindee Grant, how many versions of the same page is a wife supposed to read? Thanks, you read them all.

Doris McKay, your willingness to seek and correct my errors is greatly appreciated.

Kelly Mack, your enjoyment in reading these books has encouraged me more than you know. I am not sure that "Emeraldsea: Sunrise" would be finished even now, had it not been for the pleasant reminders that you "can't wait to read the next book". Thank you.

My late mother, **Odette Nicole Grant**, who taught me the love of books and the enjoyment of imagination.

Blessings,
R

Table of Contents

CHAPTER 1
The Storm

"No, no, I won't," screamed Cilantra as great, fat hands moved closer to her head. "You can't, you can't," she cried, hopelessly.

Unable to move her arms or legs, she watched helplessly as the hands forced a rough leather bag over her head.

The stench within the bag caused her to retch uncontrollably.

With her last breath she shouted, "Falcon, help me!"

Her head jerked left then right. Her arms and legs twitched slightly. She felt cold moist air upon her face and slowly opened her eyes.

Cilantra breathed deeply and peered through the darkness of the terrace on which she slept.

"It's only a dream," she sighed, closing her eyes once again; "Only a dream."

Laying her head back onto an overstuffed pillow, Cilantra returned to a fitful sleep.

Rain pounded incessantly, furiously. Endless sheets of water cascaded over the covered terraces of Rhala'nn's palace.

Prince Rhala'nn was the spoiled, impatient heir to the throne. His father, King Ahala'nn, was ruler of a desert kingdom named Saalespor, populated by a foul smelling people named Saalesporco; "Porco" for short. The King had long turned a blind eye to the needs of his people and to his son's ambitions, appetites and cruelty.

Lightning flashed, thunder echoed down deserted hallways and the rain redoubled its unrelenting torrent. It seemed a lifetime since the desert kingdom had seen the sun. In reality, the freak storm had raged for only a few weeks; a lifetime, however, for Cilantra.

Twelve unfortunate women had arrived in the eye of the storm. The calm blue skies that graced the harbor on that day belied the stormy turmoil in the hearts and minds of the captives.

The women disembarked a slaver called *The Black Claw,* a tall ship brig, and were led to the prince's palace during one brief lull in the tempest. Since then, stinging, wind-whipped rain, lightning and thunder assaulted both great and small in this corrupt, rancid kingdom.

Kidnapped from their homelands, these young women were being forced to forget their past lives and embrace a new one as consorts and perhaps wives of the prince.

Opulent rooms in one wing of the palace were dedicated to this shipment of brides-to-be. Each of the twelve had a private suite with a well-appointed bedroom, a dressing room (with an immense closet) and a sitting room with luxurious furnishings.

Few would exchange their freedom for mere affluence and comfort; at least that is what the philosophers taught. In reality, some of the new captives were already enticed by their lavish new lifestyle.

The sitting rooms each opened onto a covered terrace that offered unparalleled views of the city and the sea beyond. These rooms were now shuttered against the storm; all except one.

In the early morning darkness a solitary figure slept through a reoccurring nightmare. When awake, she sat motionless gazing from the terrace toward the sea. Cilantra had stayed in this same place for days without end. She watched the spot where she last glimpsed her hope, a sloop named *Emeraldsea*, as it sailed away.

At the side of her overstuffed chase lounge was a small table that held a tray and last night's meal. Like the previous lunch and breakfast before that, it remained untouched.

A sudden flash of lightning revealed a woman so striking that even the stormy darkness could not mask her beauty. Her eyes fluttered open. They were like deep, infinite pools of ebony. Tears on her porcelain-smooth skin glistened in the momentary light. Her waist length hair hung around her shoulders like a shiny black shawl.

"Cilantra," whispered a voice from the darkness behind her.

She did not move or acknowledge the voice in any way.

"Cilantra, it's me, Brittany," said the voice, a little louder.

Brittany stepped from the darkness. Her golden blond hair was woven into a thick braid that hung to the middle of her back. It was laced with golden thread and little flowers made of silver. She wore an emerald nightgown made of shimmering silk like the tent that had been her prison aboard *The Black Claw*.

Over her nightgown she wore a matching robe embroidered with tiny silver flowers. Even in the early morning gray, her remarkably green eyes sparkled bright and clear.

"Cilantra, it's me," said Brittany again.

Wrapping her arms around her knees, Cilantra pulled her legs up tightly to her chin. She looked at the lower part of the chase lounge where her legs had been and then glanced up at her friend. It was a silent invitation for Brittany to sit.

Brittany accepted the invitation. The two sat looking at one another, mournfully. Brittany tenderly took Cilantra's hands in her own. This simple act was all that was needed to release a floodgate of muted tears from them both.

In time, the mantle of silence gave way to stifled sobs and aborted words of solace.

"I thought it was all a dream; a nightmare," wept Cilantra, quietly.

With the speed of thought, her mind filled with dreadful memories of the kidnapping.

She had slipped from the Lord Hiram's encampment to enjoy a private swim away from guards and servants. Just as she stood at the river's edge an awful smell engulfed her; the first sign of hidden danger. It was the putrid smell of her Porco kidnappers which she mistook for a rotting carcass in the nearby brush.

Her husband, Lord Falcon, had warned her of the danger his family faced.

"There are enemies everywhere we go," he had said. "My father is one of the most powerful men on earth, perhaps THE most powerful." He did not say it as a boast, but as honest fact.

"You know he is a good man, but enemies are drawn to power like dragons are drawn to gold."

Gazing lovingly into her eyes, Falcon had pleaded, "Please, never go outside the camp without your guards."

Cilantra sighed as the voice and face of her husband faded from her mind.

Oh Falcon, her heart cried. *I'm so sorry.*

She shuttered as she remembered what little she could of her actual kidnapping.

Something, someone struck her from behind, pushing her face down into the river. Strong, beefy hands held her neck and head under water. Others wrapped cords around her ankles and brutally tied her hands behind her back.

Lungs screaming for air, she was finally pulled from the water. Before she could scream or even catch her breath, a dirty rag was crammed roughly into her mouth. A large, coarse body-sized sack was slipped over her head and pulled all the way down to her feet.

She felt herself being carried, over the shoulder, by some foul smelling man-beast. In just a few moments she was thrown, like a sack of tubers, into the back of some kind of wagon.

"It happened so quickly I thought it had to be a nightmare," sobbed Cilantra.

Brittany nodded and wiped a tear from her own cheek. She too knew the hopelessness of being taken by the Porco.

"The kidnappers," continued Cilantra with disjointed thoughts; "Being tied up in the wagon, the ship, the storm, The Bag, that awful bag."

Her voice trailed off into silence as she and Brittany remembered the torturous head-bag used to subdue them all.

She thought of young Coral who had almost drowned with that rough leather bag over her head. To 'teach her a lesson' she was hung from a rope behind *The Black Claw* and dragged through the sea.

The threat of such water torture was enough to insure absolute compliance from all the captives.

"On the first day here" continued Cilantra, "I watched *Emeraldsea,* and that man in the red cap, sail away. I was sure he would bring Falcon back to rescue me; us," she corrected herself.

"It was all I could think of when they introduced us to the other Favored Ones," she said.

Cilantra all but spat out the phrase used to describe women kidnapped for the prince's pleasure.

The thought of those who had been kidnapped before and how they now accepted palace life was enough to drive her back into silence.

Taking a deep breath she continued.

"I skipped dinner and snuck back here to watch." She sighed deeply. "I was so sure Falcon would come."

"I laid here and watched all night, but my husband never came. Falcon never came."

Cilantra's shoulders shook as she silently wept.

"I have stayed here, waiting and watching every day, every night since then – staring through the awful gray of this storm." Cilantra's voice trailed off into despair.

"That's enough of that," Brittany scolded, gently. "You are the wife of Lord Falcon, first born of the House of Hiram. And I am the wife of Quasar the Dragon-Slayer."

Brittany took a deep breath before continuing. "We have both survived being abducted by Porco and imprisoned in a slave ship. We sailed through a horrendous storm and are confined in the palace of a wicked prince; but we have survived!"

Momentary visions of her kidnapping flashed through her mind. She saw the Proco smashing their way into her ranch house kitchen, smelled their stench and saw Quasar being beaten. Brittany literally shook her head to clear her mind's eye.

"We fooled our jailers on the ship and avoided The Bag," whispered Brittany.

"We have survived," repeated Brittany, "And we shall survive until we are free!"

There was a new tone to Brittany's voice. Strength had replaced weakness, courage had dispelled despair.

At the sound of her voice, Cilantra looked toward her friend. Brittany was standing facing the window and the sea beyond. There was new fire in her eyes and a blush about her cheeks.

"Look," commanded Brittany.

Cilantra stood and followed Brittany's gaze out the window.

"Sunrise!" Cilantra exclaimed.

"Yes," said Brittany; "Sunrise. It's a new day."

As they watched, the gray mist of storm fled before the fiery sunrise.

"We must hurry," said Brittany, a new urgency in her voice.

"Why?" asked Cilantra.

"First, you must eat something," said Brittany.

"What?" asked Cilantra, again. She was not yet herself.

"It would not do to have you faint from hunger, now would it?"

"Well, no. I guess not," answered Cilantra, a bit dazed. "But, why must we hurry?"

"They will be coming for the dinner trays," explained Brittany, hastily. "When they do, I want to be ready."

"Ready for what?" asked Cilantra. Strength was returning to her voice. "What are you thinking?"

"Now that the storm has ended, we're going to get out of this place."

"I like what you're thinking," exclaimed Cilantra, "but how?"

"I don't know, but first things first," answered Brittany. The urgency of her voice was contagious.

She gently pushed Cilantra toward her dressing room. "We need to get dressed and you need to eat. Then…"

The sharp sound of tinkling bells stopped Brittany in mid-sentence. She glanced at the entrance to Cilantra's suite. The sound came from down the hallway outside the door.

"They're coming!" exclaimed Brittany.

"Who?" asked Cilantra.

Without answering, Brittany stepped back onto the terrace and grabbed two oranges from the dinner tray.

"Quick, hide these," she commanded, tossing them to Cilantra.

Catching them, Cilantra could not help but wonder if these very oranges were from the citrus crates that had hid her and Brittany aboard *The Black Claw*.

Without knowing why, she pushed the fruit behind a pillow that rested on a small couch. Then, turning back to Brittany she began to speak.

"What are you doing?" was all she could manage.

She stared as Brittany broke off a few small pieces of flat bread and let them fall back onto the tray. She then picked up a small teapot from the tray and carefully poured its contents into a large potted plant that was on the terrace.

"What are you doing?" Cilantra repeated.

With nimble fingers, Brittany set the teapot down and liberated a few pieces of roasted meat that were impaled on a thin stick. These she wrapped in a piece of flat bread adding a little cheese and roasted onions from the tray. The remainder of the bread Brittany shoved into the potted plant.

The sound of tinkling bells grew louder, closer.

Brittany hurried to where Cilantra stood.

"Eat this," whispered Brittany as she handed Cilantra the bread and meat. Without knowing it, she may very well have invented the sandwich.

Brittany pushed Cilantra toward the dressing room and added, "Change into hiking clothes – hurry!"

With that, Brittany bounded across the room and through the inner doorway that connected the two suites. As she silently closed the inner door, she heard the door to the hallway open and the deep voice of a man clearing his throat.

A tall, muscular man stepped from the hallway and into the room. He was dressed in colorful silk. Behind him came his youngest daughter, Lee'a. She had little bells hanging from the hem of her skirt. They jingled whenever she moved, thus announcing her presence wherever she went.

The man was named Kuubow. He was in charge of the Favored Ones. Kuubow carried a stick that was as tall as he. It was made of ornately carved wood and topped with a gold ball encrusted with jewels. As he walked across the room the stick made a slight tap each time it struck the floor. Blind, Kuubow used the sound to find his way.

Lee'a darted past her father and entered the terrace where she had left the dinner tray the night before. She smiled when she saw that Cilantra was no longer on the chase lounge.

Lee'a quickly surveyed the table and terrace and giggled a little to herself. With practiced hands the young girl picked up the tray and moved to where her father stood.

"And so?" asked the man quietly, as if he were in the middle of a sentence.

"She pretends to eat," said Lee'a in a whisper.

"How so?" asked the man.

"The teapot is empty, but the cup is unused," answered Lee'a.

She did not mention that tea-colored liquid was seeping from the bottom of the potted plant.

"Also, the oranges are gone, but no peels were left." Lee'a smiled as if it were all a game. "Nobody eats orange peels do they, PaPa?"

Just then, Cilantra stepped from the dressing room fully dressed and finishing a last bite of bread and meat. She moved with the quiet grace and confidence of one from the House of Hiram.

"It is good to see you, Kuubow," said Cilantra smoothly. "And you too, Lee'a," she added, sincerely.

Saying nothing, Lee'a set down the tray and moved to the potted plant on the terrace. There she knelt and quickly cleaned up the tea.

"I am glad you are well," answered Kuubow. He smiled broadly, revealing impossibly white teeth.

Kuubow turned slightly at the sound of the inner connecting door. Brittany stood at the opened door and asked, "May I come in?"

"Yes, of course," answered Cilantra, totally in control. She was once again her old self; confident, poised, strong and beautiful.

"Breakfast will be served in the Women's Hall," said Kuubow to them both. "Meet Lee'a and the others in the hallway as quickly as possible." It was a command, but couched in gentleness. "She will show you the way."

With that, Kuubow turned and left the room. He moved as if he could see perfectly, aided only by the tap of his stick.

Lee'a quickly picked up the dinner tray and followed her father out the door. She paused momentarily in the hallway. Turning toward Brittany and Cilantra, she smiled brightly and said, "I'll meet you out here in just a few minutes."

Still holding the dinner tray, she nimbly closed the door with her foot.

ଔ   ଔ   ଔ   ଔ   ଔ

Lord Falcon finished dressing then turned his attention to breakfast. The simple fare was delivered to his cabin at the same time each morning; sunrise. This morning it consisted of hot tea, a wedge of cheese, dense brown bread with honey and a roasted egg. It was the same breakfast enjoyed by each man aboard the brig *Fyrmatus*.

As the eldest son of the Lord Hiram, Falcon could have special food and drink reserved only for him. It was not his way. Falcon treated his men honorably, fairly. In return, his men eagerly did anything he asked of them, including die. They shared a respect found only among those who faced danger together.

The Reds, as they were known, were the fiercest soldiers in the House of Hiram. They were first in battle and often the first to shed blood. The red color of their uniforms was designed to mask wounds they might suffer. They would never show any weakness to their enemy, even when dying. To become one of the Reds was the greatest honor a soldier in the House of Hiram could hope to attain.

Lord Falcon tore off a piece of bread, careful not drip honey on his smart red uniform, and ate it eagerly. He followed that with a bite of cheese and a drink of tea. Absentmindedly, Falcon peeled off the top of the egg. Steam curled its way around his fingers.

There must be something more, he thought. *What else can I be doing?*

Falcon sighed and picked up the egg. Holding it to his lips like a tiny goblet, he tossed back his head and let the hot golden yolk flow into his mouth.

I must find Cilantra, he thought, frustration burning in his mind.

It had been weeks since his wife went missing. Well he knew that the longer she was missing the less chance he had of finding her.

Falcon's brother, Reed, commanded a spy network known as the Greens. As soon as Reed had learned that Cilantra was missing he ordered his men to find out where she had been taken and by whom.

They traced the kidnappers to the port city of Mecenas, but Falcon arrived too late. A slaver named *The Black Claw* had left port just hours before *Fyrmatus* arrived. Falcon suspected that Cilantra was aboard *The Black Claw.*

Without waiting for the rest of his father's fleet, Falcon sailed after the mystery ship. He even left port against the tide; his men straining at the oars to bring *Fyrmatus* into open sea.

Unfortunately, ever since Falcon left Mecenas his energies had been spent fighting a storm instead of the kidnappers.

Falcon poured steaming tea into his mug and brought it to his lips. The vapor swirled around his face and warmed his nostrils. He smiled as it brought to mind the only good thing to happen thus far.

A chance encounter with the sloop *Emeraldsea* provided confirmation of Cilantra's fate and an unexpected reunion with his comrades Quasar and Nemo. They often shared hopes and thoughts over tea.

Besides members of the House of Hiram, Falcon could think of no one else he would rather see in time of need.

This reunion also brought with it the unwelcomed news that Quasar's bride, Brittany had also been kidnapped.

They will strengthen each other, Falcon told himself.

As he drained the mug he glanced out of the small window in his cabin. What he saw brought a smile to his lips and, for a moment, erased the worry from his heart. On the horizon, rays of sunlight pierced the gray retreating storm.

"Sunrise!" Falcon exclaimed. "Today will be the day!"

Suddenly, Falcon thought he saw a momentary shadow cross the rising sun. He pressed close to the window to make sure, then, hope and fear dueling in his heart, ran from the cabin.

"All hands on deck!"

"All hands on deck!" shouted Falcon as he raced up the steps that lead to the quarterdeck.

Hearing Lord Falcon's order, the First Mate quickly moved to the steps. On a thick post at the top of the steps was mounted a bell. Mr. Schooper rang the bell briskly and shouted,

"All hands on deck!"

"All hands on deck!"

In moments, the deck of *Fyrmatus* was filled with sailors running to their stations.

Seconds later Falcon and the First Mate were joined on the quarterdeck by Captain Lewis, Quasar and Nemo.

The captain must have also been eating breakfast because he still had a bright white napkin hanging from his collar over the front of his uniform.

Seeing the napkin, Lord Falcon smiled slightly, but turned his head to look at anything other than the napkin. Falcon always tried to preserve the respect each man was due.

Mr. Schooper tried signaling the Captain with his eyes and then with subtle hand gestures. Captain Lewis tilted his head slightly and looked curiously at his First Mate. He took a step closer to Lord Falcon and cleared his throat as if he were about to speak.

Nemo sighed, then reached up to the Captain's collar and snatched away the napkin. Quasar looked down trying to mask the surprise of his best friend's boldness.

Captain Lewis' words caught in his throat and he turned several shades of red. Recovering quickly, he was about to ask about the alarm, when Falcon turned and pointed to the sunrise.

"Captain", said Falcon loudly. "I saw the mast of a ship sail across the rising sun."

All five men looked intently at the fiery ball hovering above the horizon. No mast, no ship, nothing was silhouetted against the sun.

Without hesitation Captain Lewis shouted, "Come to course one-one-five, Mr. Schooper!"

"Coming to course one-one-five, sir," answered Mr. Schooper.

The helmsman turned the ship's wheel, stopping it to direct the ship to course "115".

The ship responded by turning and sailing directly at the rising sun.

In a short time, the first mate shouted, "Sir, steady on course one-one-five, sir."

Very well, Mr Schooper," replied the captain. "Steady as she goes!"

"Aye, sir," shouted the First Mate. "Steady as she goes."

Still no mast, no ship, nor anything else was silhouetted against the sun.

"A double watch above, Mr. Schooper", ordered Captain Lewis.

"Aye, sir," shouted the First Mate. "A double watch it is."

"Double watch to the crow's nest," shouted Mr. Schooper.

As he watched, two sailors quickly scampered up the main mast to its very top where a platform and railing were built. The men were dressed in the dark blue uniform of Lord Norrom, sixth son of the Lord Hiram and Admiral of the fleet. High upon the mast, they could barely be seen against the sky.

As soon as the sailors had tied themselves to the top of the mast, the First Mate shouted, "Sir, double watch posted, sir."

"Very well, Mr. Schooper," replied the captain. "Sing out if they see anything, and sharp's the word!"

"Aye, sir," replied the First Mate; "Sharp's the word."

The First Mate glanced down from the quarterdeck toward three seamen busily coiling rope. They met his eyes as he nodded toward the rising sun. Immediately, all three set down their ropes and ran to the eastern most side of the bow. They, too, were now on lookout duty, and knew to keep a sharp eye for anything on the horizon.

Lord Falcon stood on the quarterdeck facing the sunrise, hands clasped behind his back. If there was any doubt in his mind that he had indeed seen a ship silhouetted against the rising sun, his face did not betray it. Jaw clenched, eyes wide, he was the very image of confidence.

Internally, however, he felt helpless and weak. Without moving his lips or bowing his head Lord Falcon, first born of the House of Hiram, uttered an earnest prayer. He humbly asked for the safe return of Cilantra and Brittany and for the wisdom to know how to make it happen. He took a deep breath, imagining that the wind blowing on his face carried his prayer to heaven.

Captain Lewis approached Falcon and stood patiently waiting for the customary acknowledgment from his commander. None came; not a nod or a glance. Finally, he spoke with a confidence that he did not feel:

"Lord Falcon, all hands are on deck. We sail on a course directly toward the sunrise. A double watch is in the crow's nest, and three on the bow. If there's a ship out there, we will find her, sir."

"That's a big 'IF', isn't it Captain?" said Falcon, quietly. He turned, toward the Captain.

"No, no, sir," stammered Captain Lewis. "That's not what I meant. There is no 'IF'. There is no doubt. There is a ship out there and we will find her, sir."

"Very good, Captain," said Falcon, forcing a reassuring smile and nodding a little; "Understood."

"Thank you, sir," replied Captain Lewis, as he turned to leave. Then, pausing, he took a deep breath and turned back to face the Lord Falcon, again.

"Sir, just one more thing?'

"What is it, Captain?" Falcon asked.

Captain Lewis looked Falcon straight in the eyes.

"We will find her, sir," said Captain Lewis, boldly. "Your wife I mean. We will get her back, safe and sound. We will, sir." Then nodding at Quasar, he added, "And your wife too, sir."

Falcon and Quasar smiled at the Captain's solemn words and worried face. Such loyalty cannot be bought or forced. It comes only in response to love, respect and humble leadership.

Falcon put his strong hand on the Captain's shoulder saying,

"Yes, my friend, we will – God willing, we will find them safe and sound."

As he spoke, a shout came loud and clear from the crow's nest.

"Ship ho!" cried a sailor from above.

"Ship ho, dead ahead!" shouted the other lookout.

All the men on deck and on the quarterdeck turned to face the sunrise. Sure enough, the masts and sails of a tall ship could clearly be seen silhouetted against the brilliant rising orb. As they watched, the ship grew larger and larger as she came wholly into view.

Suddenly, Falcon realized that the ship was on a course leading directly toward *Fyrmatus* with all her sails unfurled and full of wind.

Lord Falcon grasped the railing of the quarterdeck and leaned forward, willing himself to get as clear a view as he could. He had expected to merely spot the ship and then give chase.

"Very good, then," he said as if speaking to *The Black Claw*, "If its battle you want, then battle you shall have."

Lord Falcon turned to Captain Lewis.

"Battle stations, Captain." His order was so calm it was eerie.

"Mr. Schooper!" cried the captain, loudly. "Let's show these kidnapping cowards what the House of Hiram has to offer!"

He glanced briefly toward Quasar and Nemo, and then shouted, "Battle stations, Mr. Schooper; battle stations!"

"Aye Aye, sir," cried the First Mate as he ran to the bell.

"All hands, battle stations!" shouted Mr. Schooper as he furiously rang the bell.

"All hands, battle stations!"

Instantly, from below deck, streams of the Reds poured onto the deck. Teams of the Reds hauled up weapons that looked like giant crossbows. Sailors, too, ran to fetch other weapons and prepare the ship for battle.

Above the sound of countless soldiers and sailors running on deck came a loud voice from the crow's nest.

"Ship ho,"came the cry from above!

"Ship ho, ship ho!"

Quasar, Nemo and Falcon looked up at the crow's nest.

Don't they know their first sighting has been heard, thought Falcon? *No, that can't be it.*

Lord Falcon could clearly see both lookouts pointing and gesturing toward the sun.

"Ship ho, ship ho!" they both cried again.

Falcon quickly turned to again look at *The Black Claw* and the rising sun behind her. To his unhappy surprise, another ship could clearly be seen sailing into view.

The lookouts kept shouting, "Ship ho, ship ho!"

Before Falcon could say a word, a third and a fourth ship crossed the horizon. They both had all sails unfurled and full of wind. The four ships sailed straight for *Fyrmatus*.

CHAPTER 2
The City

$\mathcal{T}$he Women's Hall echoed with the sound of lively banter, laughter and clinking dishes. That all changed to hushed whispers as Lee'a walked in followed by the twelve new captives. They came bravely, heads held high, walking in two lines led by Cilantra and Brittany. The twelve were dressed in hardy hiking clothes rather than the flowing silks usually worn in the palace.

At the sound of his daughter's tinkling dress, Kuubow turned toward the great doors and listened. The room became deathly still. Only the jingling bells could be heard.

"You are late," said Kuubow, not unkindly.

"I am sorry, Father," said Lee'a with head bowed.

"It is our fault," announced Cilantra in a strong, confident voice. "We took longer to dress than Lee'a expected."

Cilantra offered no apology.

Kuubow motioned with his staff toward long tables that were filled with food and the other Favored Ones

"Come, eat," he said simply.

Cilantra and Brittany led the twelve to take open seats around the tables. They sat together at a table nearest the great doors. Lee'a stood motionless, watching, waiting, fear in her eyes.

As the line of women passed Kuubow he turned his head slightly in surprise and listened carefully. Instead of the expected swish of silk he heard the distinct sound of cotton trousers and leather shoes.

Kuubow took a step or two toward Lee'a.

"Why are they dressed for hiking," he asked quietly?

He was stopped by the commanding voice of Cilantra. Being married to the first born of the House of Hiram, she knew how to speak with authority when needed.

"It is a beautiful day, Kuubow," declared Cilantra. "We would make use of it."

Smiling charmingly, she continued speaking with her sweetest voice.

"Please arrange for us to take a walking tour of Prince Rhala'nn's magnificent city. I'm sure he is so proud. We must see it all."

Kuubow stood motionless. He was totally unprepared for this turn of events. Never before had Favored Ones acted like this.

Suddenly, Kuubow became aware that the room was totally still. Though blind himself, he knew all eyes must be on him, watching, and waiting.

Kuubow smiled broadly, displaying his beautiful white teeth, and said for all to hear,

"Well done, Lee'a."

His daughter almost fainted at the sound of her name.

"Finish the arrangements I made with the guards. Tell them they will have thirteen guests on a walking tour."

"Thirteen?" asked Lee'a, unsure of what was happening.

She knew of no arrangements with the palace guards. In fact, none had been made. Kuubow was trying hard to save face.

"Yes, of course," answered her father with a kindly laugh. "Don't you remember? You, too, are to go with them. It is time for you, as well, to see what lies beyond the palace walls."

The Women's Hall erupted in wonder-filled conversation. All of the other Favored Ones spoke at the same time, staring and gesturing at the twelve.

Cilantra glanced at Brittany who was sitting directly across the table from her. With a wink and a smile she helped herself to a serving of fruit and breakfast bread. Brittany smiled back and did likewise.

Armonia, Maria, Petrea, Coral, and the rest of the twelve looked at one another and collectively sighed in relief. Coral was especially surprised the plan had worked. She was sitting right next to Brittany and trembled visibly.

"I'm sorry. I can't help it," she whispered when Brittany squeezed her hand.

Brittany handed Coral the last roasted egg.

"Here, you eat this." Brittany said gently.

"I can't; you eat it," replied Coral.

"Eat!" said Brittany. Her voice was quiet, but there was a no-nonsense quality about it.

Maria giggled nervously as she watched Petrea spear a sausage with her fork. It was her third sausage, and the last on the platter.

Armonia leaned in toward Petrea.

"You better be careful," warned Armonia. "They're all watching."

"What?" replied Petrea, defensively. "That guy told us to eat, so I'm eating! What's wrong with that?"

As if in response to Armonia's warning, Petrea reached across the table and took a large piece of breakfast bread. She broke it into two smaller pieces and wrapped them around the sausage. Taking a large bite, Petrea said,

"These are great, you should try one."

Armonia shook her head, unhappily.

"I would, but you took the last one," she said and then looked away.

"Don't talk with your mouth full," laughed Maria.

Petrea glared defiantly at both of them.

Cilantra carefully surveyed the interaction of her eleven friends and smiled.

This is going to be an interesting day, she thought.

Looking around the hall, Cilantra realized Kuubow and Lee'a were gone.

A very interesting day, she thought again.

Suddenly, Cilantra felt a presence standing behind her. At the same time, she noticed Brittany was staring with a strange expression.

She turned her head to find one of the original Favored Ones standing behind her holding two platters.

"Egg, sausage," asked the girl as she extended the platters toward Cilantra?

"Oh," exclaimed Cilantra. "Thank you."

Cilantra quickly glanced around the room. No one seemed to notice or care.

Motioning to an empty chair next to her she asked, "Would you like to sit?"

Taking the platters and placing them on the table, she continued, "My name is Cilantra."

"I'm Corree," said the girl smiling. "Yes, I would love to; Thank you."

As she bent to sit in the chair her head came close to Cilanta. Whispering, she said, "You must be careful."

Then, she slid into the chair, smiling for all the world to see.

Cilantra took an egg and gestured to Brittany. "Would you like an egg?"

Brittany's eyes shifted from Cilantra to Corree and then back to Cilantra.

"Why thank you," she said, a little too loudly.

Corree spoke quickly, quietly, barely moving her lips.

"I was one of the first taken. I've been here two years and have never left the palace. I want to come, too."

"Two years!" exclaimed Brittany and Cilantra at the same time.

"Shhhh," warned Corree. She looked around the room, cautiously.

Suddenly, Corree laughed as if Brittany and Cilantra had said something funny. She looked around the room, again and then continued quietly.

"There were three others with me at first, but they're gone now."

She paused then said sadly, "I think they displeased the prince."

A shadow crossed Corree's face as she spoke. "None of us has ever left the palace. I want to come, too."

Without another word, Corree rose, left the table and casually walked out of the Women's Hall.

Brittany and Cilantra watched her go, unsure of what to say or do. Moments later, they saw Lee'a enter the Women's Hall wearing hiking clothes very much like those worn by Brittany, Cilantra and the others.

They looked away when they saw Lee'a. They needed to make plans. Things were going much faster than expected.

Cilantra was about to speak when she saw Brittany signal by slightly shaking her head.

Turning, Cilantra found that Lee'a was standing directly behind her, waiting silently.

"Oh Lee'a," exclaimed Cilantra a little too cheerfully. "You've changed clothes."

"When you are finished eating, I will take you to the guards," said Lee'a politely. "They will take us on a tour of the city as you requested."

Try as she might, Lee'a could not mask the excitement and fear she was feeling.

Trying to act as if nothing was unusual, Cilantra casually drank some tea and daintily wiped her mouth with a napkin.

"Thank you, Lee'a," replied Cilantra sweetly. "I think we are all just about ready to go."

Cilantra and Brittany slowly stood, looking around the table at the others.

"Ladies," declared Cilantra. "Let's not keep the guards waiting."

With that, she carefully folded her napkin and placed it on the table. Brittany and the others did likewise, except for Petrea.

"Just wait a minute," said Petrea with her mouth full of food. "I've got one more bite of sausage."

As if she had not heard Petrea, Cilantra left the table and casually followed Lee'a toward the great doors. Brittany and Coral did likewise, trailed by the others. Petrea came last.

As they passed through the great doors and into the hallway, the Women's Hall detonated with a blast of conversation.

ಜ   ಜ   ಜ   ಜ   ಜ

"Ship ho, ship ho!" the lookouts cried again.

Falcon continued to face the sunrise and the oncoming armada as lookouts shouted, "Ship ho, ship ho!"

Captain Lewis approached him and patiently stood awaiting orders.

"How many, Captain," asked Falcon?

"Sir?" replied the captain.

He was unsure of what Lord Falcon was actually asking. In the tenseness of the moment, he did not want to make a mistake.

"What is your count, Captain?" said Falcon, strain showing in his voice. "How many ships do you see?"

Captain Lewis turned to fully face the sunrise and count the ships that were headed for *Fyrmatus.*

"I count seven ships, sir," replied the captain; "*The Black Claw* and six others behind her."

From above a lookout cried, "Ship ho, ship ho!"

"Make that eight," said Quasar with a gloom-filled voice. He grimaced as a new ship crossed the horizon and came into view.

Quasar, Nemo, Falcon and Captain Lewis stood facing the sun and recounted the ships crossing the horizon.

"What are your orders, sir?" asked the captain; sure he already knew the answer.

"Two, perhaps three, but not eight," said Falcon, quietly. "Not eight."

"*Fyrmatus* is a fine ship, sir; and the crew, there's none, better." replied the captain.

He took a deep breath and continued.

"But eight ships, sir. We can't repel eight ships, and we certainly can't board 'em all."

Lord Falcon leaned as far over the railing as his arms could bear. It was as if he was willing himself closer to the oncoming warships.

Captain Lewis waited for Lord Falcon's orders, but Falcon only stared out at the horizon.

Finally, feeling he could wait no longer, the captain shouted his own orders; the only order he thought possible.

"Mr. Schooper, come about! Reverse course," cried the captain.

"Aye, sir," replied the First Mate; "Coming about."

Lord Falcon turned hotly toward the captain, shock and rage burning on his face.

"Belay that order, Mr. Schooper!" screamed Falcon to the First Mate.

Then, with eyes like steel and a strangely restrained voice he added, "Steady as she goes, Captain."

Quasar and Nemo wished they were anywhere other than on the quarterdeck at this moment. They tactfully moved away toward the helm.

Only the captain's years of experience enabled him to continue. He had never before made such an error in judgment and protocol.

"Steady as she goes, Mr. Schooper," cried the captain. His voice did not betray the wave of nausea that had overtaken him.

"Aye, sir," repeated the First Mate, sounding confused. "Maintaining course; steady as she goes."

The captain was about to apologize to Lord Falcon, when he was stopped short by Falcon's expression. His eyes were afire, his jaw firmly set and his shoulders straight and strong.

"Captain Lewis," commanded Lord Falcon in slow, measured, words. "Hoist the battle flag!"

If Falcon had any doubt or misgiving, neither his face nor his voice revealed it.

"Aye, sir," replied the captain, smoothly. "The battle flag it is."

Looking down from the quarterdeck to a sailor below, Captain Lewis shouted, "Hoist the battle flag!"

"Aye, sir." replied the sailor running to a chest that held the flag.

"What is happening," Quasar asked of no one in particular? No one in particular replied.

Quasar and Nemo moved closer to the captain and Lord Falcon.

"What is happening," Quasar asked again?

Captain Lewis had already made one colossal error; he was not about to risk making another by saying more than Falcon wanted.

Falcon, for his part said nothing, but stared silently out to sea.

Nemo put a strong hand on Quasar's shoulder and said, "Your time will come. But now, strength will be seen in patience."

Quasar, closed his eyes, breathed deeply, but said nothing.

In moments, a huge flag featuring Twin Black Hawks on a field of red ascended the main mast. As it rose aloft, the ship's full company cheered as one voice.

Lord Falcon smiled proudly at the sight of the Twin Black Hawks, emblem of the House of

Hiram. He turned once again to face the rising sun and the oncoming ships. Captain Lewis, Quasar and Nemo followed Falcon's gaze.

As if in response to the battle flag on *Fyrmatus*, *The Black Claw* hoisted a halyard with a set of signal flags.

In almost total unison, battle flags were hoisted on the masts of the oncoming ships. Captain Lewis looked in amazement, leaned on the railing, and looked again.

"Falcon! Falcon!" shouted Nemo, unhelpfully. It was all that would come out of his mouth at the sight of the battle flags.

"My Lord," proclaimed Captain Lewis in as controlled a voice as he could manage, "It's not *The Black Claw*, sir."

"Aye, Captain, I know," answered Falcon grinning like a little boy. "It's not *The Black Claw*, it is *Celantra* followed by *Gauntlet* and *Sea Core*.

Falcon, Quasar, Nemo and Captain Lewis shouted happily and slapped one another's backs.

"Look," cried Falcon, *"Celantra* flies the Twin Black Hawks on a sky blue field. My brother Herald is onboard."

"He raised the signal flags!" added Nemo.

"Of course he did," added Quasar as he looked at the ship. "Who else would it be?"

Quasar smiled to himself.

"*The Black Claw* is not *The Black Claw*," he said, laughing in relief. "It's *Celantra*, and Lord *Herald* is signaling his brothers!"

"*Gauntlet* flies the Hawks on a wine-colored flag," shouted Falcon. "It's got to be my brother Vine,"

"Vine's Wines" shouted Nemo; "Vine's Wines!"

For a moment he was transported back to happier days when he and Quasar had first met Gannon; youngest brother in the House of Hiram. Nemo smiled wistfully as he remembered meeting the ten brothers and the Lord Hiram, himself.

"Look, look!" shouted Nemo, suddenly. He almost danced with excitement as he pointed at the ships.

Each of the eight ships now flew flags displaying the Twin Black Hawks of the House of Hiram.

Regaining his composure, Captain Lewis shouted, "Sir, I see the *Advocate* and behind her the *Adventurer*. I can't make out the others just yet."

"Aye, Captain," answered Falcon, his voice full of excitement.

Advocate flies the forest green banner of my brother Reed. And behind her *Adventurer* flies the Hawks on a field of yellow.

"That can only be Shank," shouted Nemo, "and his men. I'd wager on it.

"I hope so," said Quasar, smiling. "A ship full of archers would be a handy thing to have."

The four men watched in amazed silence as the remaining ships grew in size and were recognized.

"It's the *Valiant!*" shouted Nemo. "Tulmar must be aboard her."

"How can you tell," asked Captain Lewis? "I can't see her flag. It flies right in front of the sun."

"That's just it. Don't you see," replied Nemo, good-naturedly? "Tulmar's color is fire orange; the same color as the sun. It's Tulmar, it must be!"

"Well, I can see what's behind *Valiant,*" shouted Captain Lewis; "*Tempest!* And she flies the Hawks on a purple field," declared the captain with confidence.

"That's Ram!" declared Falcon. "And he's brought a ship full of war machines. I just know it!"

"Falcon?" cried Nemo, alarmed. "There's a ship that flies the Hawks on a silver field."

"Aye, there is," answered Falcon, sadly.

"But, that's Kyler's color" said Nemo, confused. "He fell at the Battle of Three Rivers!"

"Aye, he did," replied Falcon.

A dark cloud passed behind Falcon's eyes as he remembered the fiery death of his brother, Kyler.

"It is his ship, *Trident*, bearing his flag," explained Falcon. "Most of his lancers died with him," continued Falcon, painfully. "But some survived the dragons' breath at Three Rivers."

Falcon looked long and hard at *Trident*. "They have trained more lancers and horses," he said gloomily. "The Silvers have not yet seen battle, except those few who survived Three Rivers."

For a moment, Falcon's mind retreated into some deep dark place.

"The *Trident* was built expressly to carry the horses and the men that make up the Silvers," he said with a voice void of emotion. "They will honor Kyler, or die trying."

Nemo regretted saying anything at all.

"Lord Falcon," said the captain, breaking the dark silence that had descended upon them. "There's one more ship, but she's unknown to me."

All four again turned their attention to the horizon and the speck of a ship that had revealed herself.

"I thought I knew all the ships in the Lord Hiram's navy," said Captain Lewis, peeved with himself.

"Maybe its Gannon," said Nemo. "Does Gannon have a ship, now,?" asked Nemo.

He longed to see his friend and hoped desperately that this ninth ship would fly Gannon's striped flag. His words went unanswered.

As they watched, the ship began to take form. She was larger than the others and had extra sails, too. In but a few moments, her battle flag would come into view. The four strained to see the colors.

Lord Falcon slowly stood straighter. He unconsciously pulled his shoulders back and buttoned the top button of his jacket.

Captain Lewis, Quasar and Nemo drew in deep breaths at the same time.

"The ninth ship is *Vengeance*," declared Lord Falcon. His voice was filled with awe.

"She flies Twin Black Hawks on a field of gold," he said simply, and then added; "My father has come!"

Lord Falcon turned from the sea back to the quarterdeck. Captain Lewis, Quasar and Nemo all faced him. Falcon smiled the watchful smile of a seasoned warrior.

"We have found the fleet," said Falcon, in a voice strong like steel. "Now it's time to find our wives."

CHAPTER 3
The Sea

"*L*ower another drogue," order Lord Falcon.

"Aye, sir," replied Captain Lewis; "Lowering another drogue."

"Mr. Schooper," shouted the captain. "Lower drogue three."

"Drogue three away," shouted Mr. Schooper.

A third drogue was lowered from the stern of the ship as *Celantra* approached *Fyrmatus*.

"What is he doing?" asked Nemo of the helmsman.

Surprised, the helmsman looked around to make sure Nemo wasn't talking to someone else before daring to answer.

"He's slowing the ship so *Celantra* can safely come along side."

Nemo nodded as if he understood, but he didn't really. Then, in his mind he heard his father's voice: *Remember the key to learning. An ignorant man pretends to know what he does not know. A learned man admits it and learns all the more.*

Nemo stopped nodding his head and spoke the key to learning.

"I don't understand."

"A drogue is a large round basket lined with sailcloth," explained the helmsman.

He nodded toward a fourth drogue lying sideways on the quarterdeck. Three cords were attached evenly around the opening of the basket. These were tied to a line that was secured to the stern of the ship.

"The basket is lowered with the opening facing the back of the ship." The helmsman used words that Nemo could understand.

"When lowered into the sea," continued the helmsman, "water trapped in the basket creates a drag on the ship and so slows the speed of the ship."

Nemo again nodded his head, but this time he really did understand.

"So the more drogues you lower, the slower the ship," replied Nemo.

"Exactly," answered the helmsman with a smile.

"Lower the sheets, Mr. Schooper. And stay the jib" cried Captain Lewis.

"Aye, Captain," replied the First Mate. "Lower the sheets and stay the jib." shouted the First Mate.

Immediately, sailors swarmed up the masts and pulled in all the sails except for one at the bow of the ship.

Nemo saw the same thing was happening on *Celantra*. In a few moments, both ships sailed slowly alongside one another.

Cupping his hands, Lord Falcon shouted, "Ahoy *Celantra*. What news?"

From the quarterdeck of *Celantra* came the reply.

"Ahoy *Fyrmatus*."

Nemo smiled at the familiar voice of Lord Herald, fifth son of the House Hiram.

"The Lord Hiram greets thee," cried Herald, formally; then, with a smile in his voice continued. "Are you well, brother?"

"I will be," replied Falcon, "when Cilantra is again by my side."

And Brittany by mine, said Quasar to himself.

Smiling, Falcon added, "It's good to see you, brother."

There was no more time for pleasantries.

"The Lord Hiram has called a counsel of war," shouted Herald.

"Out here," asked Falcon?

"Aboard his ship," answered Herald.

"Why then is *Vengeance* sailing so far back," asked Falcon?

Quasar and Nemo could not help looking out toward the skyline. Even now, the Lord Hiram's ship was far away from the others, sailing almost parallel to the horizon.

"*Vengeance* will be here soon enough," shouted Herald. "When she comes, we will all board her." He sounded like a prophet.

As he spoke, *Celantra* hoisted a halyard with a set of signal flags. In moments, *Vengeance* changed course and headed straight for the rest of the fleet.

Quasar and Nemo stood motionless, except for the sway and heave of *Fyrmatus*. They were entranced at the sight of the Lord Hiram's ship coming upon them. Quasar squinted and leaned out over the railing to get a better view.

"Look, look!" shouted Nemo.

His mind had much to say as he pointed to the horizon, but his mouth would only repeat, "look, look!"

Lord Falcon, Captain Lewis, Mr. Schooper and even the helmsman looked to where Nemo pointed.

As *Vengeance* turned toward the fleet she exposed another ship crossing the horizon behind her. Time seemed to stop on the quarterdeck as everyone watched the new ship in stunned silence.

"It is *Scorpion*," shouted Herald from *Celantra*, answering the as yet unasked question.

"Until now, *Vengeance* has protected her and kept her as far away from the fleet as possible," continued Herald. "She carries a very special passenger."

CB   CB   CB   CB   CB

Lee'a quickly navigated a labyrinth of corridors and passageways. In just a few minutes she led the group out into the Woman's Garden. It was the very same garden through which they had entered the palace on the day they arrived.

The girls all smiled at the beauty of the garden.

After the recent rains, the fountains were full, the grass lush and all the leaves were washed and shiny. Even the shrubberies were free of the desert dust that usually coated their leaves. Flowering plants added bright colors and sweet scents wherever the girls walked.

Lee'a moved quickly. She was not willing to stop and admire any flower, pond or view.

"I cannot, we will not, be late, please," she repeated at each request to pause. "The guards are waiting. Please come."

Lee'a marched through a flowering archway only to find that none of the girls were following. Sighing, the little girl quickly retraced her steps.

She found the twelve standing in a circle admiring a head-piece that Maria had woven from flowering vines.

"This grows at home," she heard Maria say as she placed the wreath upon her own head.

"This is your home, now," said Lee'a. A slight note of sadness seeped from her voice.

Maria had long blond hair, like Brittany, only thinner and wavy. The green vine and colored blooms on her head made her look like a bride.

Brittany smiled, remembering the day she married Quasar, but her happy memory was short lived.

From within the bushes there came a rustling sound. The girls quickly moved away and huddled together for safety. Whatever was in the bushes sounded large and dangerous.

"Are there animals in the garden?" asked Coral. Her eyes were wide in worry.

Lee'a shook her head. Ignoring the sound she said, "I cannot, we will not, be late, please. The guards are waiting. Please come." Then, smiling shyly at Maria added, "You look pretty."

She turned and moved back toward the flowering archway.

Coral jumped at another sound from the bushes. Suddenly, the worried face of Corree popped out of the shrubs.

Coral shrieked.

"Shhhh," Corree whispered, putting her finger to her lips. "I want to come, too."

"Well, hurry up then," chided Petrea without so much as a blink. "You just keep behind me. No one will notice."

Cilantra and Brittany stared at the girl.

Cilantra whispered, "We just met her at breakfast. Do you think she can be trusted?"

"How do we know anyone can be trusted?" Brittany replied, darkly. "Anyway, she's here; What can we do?"

Cilantra looked intensely into Corree's eyes and asked, "Are you sure?"

Corree nodded saying "Yes, oh yes," then repeated, "I want to come, too."

Cilantra and Brittany reluctantly agreed.

"There's nothing else to be done," said Brittany.

"Alright," replied Cilantra, then turning to Petrea asked, "Can you keep her hidden?"

"You bet," replied Petrea, confidently.

Corree moved quickly out of the bushes and slipped behind Petrea. The others protectively closed in around her.

She was dressed in the exactly the same hiking clothes as the twelve. With that, the twelve became thirteen; plus Lee'a, fourteen.

They moved quickly to catch up with Lee'a, running to get through the archway before losing sight of Kuubow's little girl.

They watched her disappear around a tall hedge. Laughing, the girls raced to be the first to turn the corner.

Stumbling to stop short, they found themselves face to face with Lee'a and five royal guards.

The guards were unlike the hideous Porco who had kidnapped them. They were tall, clean and did not smell. The guards wore red pants and thin black vests over large bare chests. Their arms bulged with muscles and their shaved heads glistened in the morning sun. They were not tattooed like the Porco kidnappers.

Coral began trembling and crying softly as she saw the guards holding head bags.

"It'll be fine, I promise," whispered Petrea, though she, too, was afraid.

She grabbed Coral's arm as much to keep her from running as passing out. As a group, the girls backed away from the guards.

"These are not the punishment bags from the ship," announced Lee'a, cheerfully.

She noticed all color had drain from Coral's face and that the others looked as if they were about to run away.

"These are Bags of Modesty," she explained, innocently.

Lee'a tried to think of words that would comfort them. For one so young, she spoke with amazing poise.

"Your faces are for the prince alone. No man may see your face and live," she explained. "You are special."

She had hoped this would encourage them. It did not. Lee'a tried to speak kindly and reassuringly. She did not understand why they all reacted so strongly to the head bags.

Coral stopped crying, but try as she might, she could not stop trembling.

"The Bags of Modesty are protection for you and for the men around you," continued Lee'a. "If a man were to see your face, he would have to pay with pain."

"What about these guards?" asked Petrea. Her tone was rough, challenging. It was not really a question.

"Some of the men in the palace are blind, like my father. His eyes were taken the day he turned thirteen, the day he became a man. If they are not blind, then they are special, like these guards."

"What do you mean, 'special'?" asked Petrea, impatiently.

Lee'a thought for a moment before answering. She didn't really know what had been done to the guards to make them special.

"You should ask my father," she said simply.

"What about the Porco who took me and killed my father?" asked Armonia, bitterly.

"You were not yet a Favored One" replied Lee'a, simply. "Seeing your face was no crime."

"Killing my father was," said Armonia.

Lowering her eyes Lee'a added, "I'm sorry about your father. I do not know much about the Spotters and the Takers."

"It's not her fault," said Brittany, gently.

"I know," replied Armonia in a horse whisper.

She tried very hard not to cry, but a single tear still made its way slowly down her cheek.

With that, Lee'a motioned to the guards who then handed a bag to each girl.

"On the ship, they forced the bags over our heads," whispered Petrea to Coral. "At least now we can put them on ourselves."

It was all the comfort she could offer.

"Do you need me to help you," Petrea asked Coral?

Coral shook her head and, taking a deep breath, put the thin soft bag over her own head. It was surprisingly light and loose fitting.

"Hey," exclaimed Petrea when she saw Coral. "Your bag sparkles!"

"So does yours," replied Coral, quietly.

The girls all started looking at one another, playfully describing the bags to each other.

Suddenly, Petrea noticed Corree crouching in the middle of the group, without a bag. She quickly removed the bag from her own head and handed it to Corree.

"Put this on," she commanded. "They won't be able to tell who you are."

Without waiting for a reply, Petrea boldly walked to a guard and extended her hand. He looked at her in surprise, but said nothing.

"I need a bag,' explained Petrea, simply.

The guard looked suspiciously at Petrea, and then turned to Lee'a.

"Your father said there are thirteen in the group," said the guard.

"That's right," answered Lee'a. She quickly looked over the group and counted one extra.

"There are thirteen in the group, and you should have thirteen bags," continued Lee'a, confidently.

"With you there are fourteen in the group, not thirteen," countered the guard.

"Yes," said Lee'a laughing lightly. "But I don't need a bag. There are thirteen who need bags."

She spoke casually and with total confidence.

Satisfied, the guard searched in his pouch and found another bag, which he handed to Petrea.

"Thank you," she said simply, and placed the bag on her head

She turned abruptly on her heals and quickly moved back to where Coral and Corree stood.

"Everything's just fine," she whispered with a grin in her voice.

Lee'a suddenly came from behind her and also whispered.

"When we are alone, you will please tell me what happened."

Petrea tried to ignore Lee'a who then added, "You can tell me, or my father."

Petrea quickly nodded her agreement.

She's awfully old for one so young, thought Petrea.

"Line up, line up," squealed Lee'a excitedly. She was, after all, a little girl leaving the palace for the first time.

Cilantra and Brittany stood nearest the guards and Lee'a. The others lined up behind them in the same order as when they were captives on *The Black Claw*, except Corree, who stood right behind Petrea.

When the Head Guard clapped his hands, the other guards took up their positions; one at the front of the line with the Head Guard, one on either side in the middle of the line and one at the rear.

"Stay close," commanded the Head Guard, "and remember who you are; Favored Ones"

Cilantra's eyes narrowed angrily, shielded from view by the head bag.

I'll always remember who I am, she thought, passionately. *I am of the House of Hiram!*

Without further comment the Head Guard turned and led the group out of the

Woman's Garden and into a dark alley that served as a hidden side entrance to the palace.

Important guests used the grand entrance to come and go to the palace, but for others, like this group, there was a common gateway.

The group found themselves walking on a shadowed stone lane. It was bordered by the walls of tall windowless buildings that stood left and right along the way. The group could not be seen or heard.

The narrow alleyway was dark, bare and totally quiet. It was so quiet that the girls all stopped talking and just stared ahead, trying to see what might be next.

The silence and shadows were eerie. The girls jumped when a large desert rat ran across their path. They squeezed together in a tight knot for safety.

Lee'a swallowed a shriek that tried to escape her throat. Subconsciously, she reached up and took Cilantra's hand in her own. Cilantra smiled sadly for the little girl.

The guards never slowed their pace, nor hastened it. They just relentlessly walked on. The girls hurried to keep up. Gone was their orderly line.

In time, they came to large double iron gates and a little hut from which immerged two very surprised and unkempt guards.

"Fools," cried the Head Guard. "Open the gates!"

The two immediately ran to the gates and unlocked them. Then, without hesitation, they pulled the great iron gates open.

"When we return," shouted the Head Guard, "see to it that we don't wait so long, or you will pay with pain."

With that, the Head Guard led the group through the gates and into the city.

The two unfortunate guards nodded apologetically and quickly closed and relocked the gates. They stood in mute wonder, watching as the group of Favored Ones disappeared down the road toward the sea.

Cilantra smiled as they proceeded through the city toward the harbor.

I can't believe we're out, she thought, silently.

Her mind began to race. *What are we going to do now?*

Panic curled its icy fingers around her heart. Cilantra took a deep breath and tried to remain calm.

One thing at a time, she reminded herself.

The buildings nearest the palace were large and ornate. High elaborate walls hid most of the courtyards and buildings from view, but through intricate metal gates the girls were able to see glimpses of unimaginable extravagance.

The road was dotted with palm trees and fountains. Horse-drawn wagons loaded with baskets and barrels lazily drove along the street. People walked to and fro in no particular hurry. Everyone, however, gave way to the palace guards and the line of Favored Ones

As they progressed down the road, Cilantra noticed that the fine buildings were replaced by more industrial ones with attached apartments. Clearly the people who lived here worked hard and lived where they worked.

Occasionally there was a shop, catering to the needs of the workers, but mostly these buildings looked like small, cramped factories with even smaller homes.

Cilantra noticed that the apartments each had a cramped yard in which grew a mulberry tree, sometimes two. The trees were filled with large green leaves and branches that were heavy with black and red berries.

Children could be seen in the yards chopping mulberry leaves and sprinkling them into shallow boxes.

"What are they doing?" asked Brittany.

"I don't know," replied Cilantra.

"Silk," answered Lee'a, simply. She was still holding tightly to Cilantra's hand.

"What," asked Cilantra and Brittany?

"The shallow boxes are filled with squirmy white silkworms," squealed Lee'a. "They feed on mulberry leaves. Everybody grows them to make silk. We have them in the Palace, too."

Cilantra and Brittany looked more carefully into the yards. Small children, older children and adults were busily working everywhere they looked.

"When the worms are ready," continued Lee'a, "the older children carefully move them to a tree branch, a shrub or a rack. That's where the worm changes into a moth cocoon."

Cilantra and Brittany could see white fuzzy pods hanging from every possible twig and stick. They could also see old women carefully reeling filaments from mature cocoons. Some twisted the filaments into silk strands. The strands were combined to make thread and the thread was wrapped around thick smooth wooden dowels.

As the group passed a large courtyard, Lee'a pointed to a great iron pot filled with boiling water. Around it, men worked in the hot steam. They washed the raw silk in the steam and boiling water. This was cruel work for those living in a desert.

The presence of the people and the brightness of the road made the girls feel less frightened. They slowly returned to walking, more or less, in their ordered line.

Everywhere the girls looked they could see long threads of silk drying in the sun. It seemed as if huge spiders had covered everything with their webs. Old women with bent gnarled hands painstakingly wrapped dried threads onto skeins.

As the girls passed, workers stopped their labors and stared. Men lowered their eyes and looked away. Children ran into the safety of their mother's arms.

The group walked on.

The road took them to an area of shops and stalls. Here, apartments were built above the ground floor businesses. The noisy buying and selling barely stopped as the group passed by, but the men still lowered they eyes.

Cilantra slowed her pace to allow more distance between herself and the two guards at the front of the line.

"We are getting near the sea," whispered Cilantra. "I can feel it in the air."

"I can smell it," replied Brittany glancing toward a stall filled with baskets of fish. She wrinkled her nose at the odor of the day-old catch.

"I can't believe we've made it this far," continued Cilantra. *One thing at a time*, she silently reminded herself.

"What are you two planning?" came a voice from behind. It was Armonia, who always seemed to be watching and listening.

Cilantra looked back at Armonia. Whether due to excitement or overconfidence, Cilantra's usual caution gave way to boldness.

"We're going to escape," she declared.

"Really?" exclaimed Armonia.

She hesitated for a moment, and then added, "Take me with you, please."

Cilantra looked toward Brittany, who nodded slightly.

"We will if we can. We will take everyone who wants to come, if there is room."

"What do you mean, 'if there is room'?" asked Armonia.

"There was a ship waiting for us in the harbor when we first arrived," explained Cilantra, quietly.

She looked toward the guards, and then lowered her voice even more.

"She is called *Emeraldsea* and was sent by my husband."

"Are you sure?" asked Armonia.

Brittany and Cilantra both nodded, confident that the *Emeraldsea* was indeed sent by Lord Falcon.

"There was a sailor on the ship. He had a red leather cap; the kind worn only by my husband's troops."

"Your husband has an army?" asked Armonia, a little too loudly.

"Do you want to come with us or not?" muttered Brittany.

Armonia nodded silently.

"Look for a boat called *Emeraldsea*," ordered Cilantra. "I think she is big enough to take all thirteen of us."

"Fourteen," said a familiar voice.

Cilantra, Brittany and Armonia jumped at the sound of Lee'a's little voice. Somehow she had moved up close to the three without being seen.

"If *Emeraldsea* can take thirteen she can take fourteen," whispered Lee'a. "Besides," she added, "I'm not very big."

"Lee'a!" all three exclaimed in surprise; they were entirely too loud.

Cilantra, Brittany, Armonia and Lee'a quickly looked at the guards. Though all seemed as it should, panic filled their hearts. Then, without warning, the Head Guard turned to face the girls. Raising his right hand he stopped the group in the shadow of the city gates.

Cilantra, Brittany Armonia and Lee'a stared at the Head Guard and tried to act casually. They failed miserably.

"I hope you have enjoyed your walk through our beautiful city," he began.

"If this is beautiful I'd hate to see dreadful," complained Petrea, a little too loudly.

Several girls giggled to themselves. The guard's eyes stared straight ahead.

"I think we're ok," whispered Brittany

"I hope so," replied Armonia.

Sounding much like a bored tour guide, The Head Guard continued.

"We will soon journey to the harbor and seashore beyond."

If he heard their comments about *Emeraldsea* or Petrea's snide remark, he showed no sign of it.

"When we return, you will be free to visit shops and stalls along the way. I have coin enough for you all to purchase whatever trinkets, blin-blin or finery that catches your eye.

An excited chatter arose from the girls. The Head Guard smiled, revealing teeth that had been filed into sharp dagger-like points.

"'The better to eat you with, my dear,'" muttered Petrea as the chatter quickly faded.

Gesturing to a shop built into the city walls, the Head Guard continued.

"Refreshments are awaiting you. Eat and drink. When you have finished, we will continue our tour."

The Head Guard nodded to two of his men. They moved into the shop, roughly emptying it of anyone doing business within.

When he thought it safe, the Head Guard motioned for the girls to enter. Two guards remained in the shop while the three others stood watch outside, blocking the door with their massive bodies.

The girls entered the shop like an invading army. They were not as interested in food or drink as they were in trinkets and blin-blin.

It was a large shop with one section that was filled with inexpensive jewelry and cosmetics. Another section displayed raw and woven silks. The shop also offered foods like breads, mulberry tarts, sweet wines, dried fish, dried figs and nuts. Tools, cords, nets and other fishing supplies hung on the walls.

Cilantra, Brittany and Armonia quickly made their way to a back corner of the shop. Partly hidden by a large loom, they were confident they could speak in private.

"Are you sure *Emeraldsea* is waiting for us?" asked Armonia excitedly.

Before Cilantra could answer, a brash familiar voice chimed in.

"What's *Emeraldsea?*" asked the voice.

The three girls quickly turned to find Petrea standing next to the loom. She was smiling impishly. Behind her they found Coral, looking better than they had ever seen. The color had returned to her face and her eyes twinkled with hope.

"What is *Emeraldsea*, if you don't mind me asking?" said Coral.

Cilantra and Brittany looked at one another as if to say, *this is really getting out of hand.*

Before Cilantra could answer either Petrea or Coral, another voice sweetly answered for her:

"*Emeraldsea* is a boat. Cilantra's husband sent it. He has an army. They wear red hats."

Cilantra, Brittany, Petrea and Coral turned toward the voice. Lee'a stepped out from behind a large sack of grain.

"And the boat is big enough to take all fourteen of us," she added, happily.

Lee'a smiled brightly; confident she remembered all that she had overheard.

"A boat?' asked Coral.

"Yes," answered Cilantra.

"An army?' asked Petrea.

"Yes," sighed Cilantra.

"Are you sure *Emeraldsea* is waiting for us?" asked Armonia for the second time.

"No," answered Cilantra, truthfully. "The last time I saw *Emeraldsea* she was sailing out of the harbor. I think she was sailing to tell my husband I am here."

Cilantra visibly shrunk under the weight of it all.

"Then the storm hit again," Cilantra continued. "I've watched day and night for *Emeraldsea* to return."

"Listen," said Brittany. "We know Lord Falcon, Cilantra's husband, sent *Emeraldsea* to rescue us. You don't have to believe us. Just don't betray us."

Armonia, Petrea, Coral and Lee'a all nodded their heads solemnly. If there was a chance of escape, they would gladly take it. No matter what, they would never betray Cilantra and Brittany to the guards.

Suddenly, a voice came from behind the loom.

"What's this all about," asked Corree?

At the sight of Corree, Cilantra put her face into her hands and shook her head slowly.

Brittany took several long breaths, not sure if she should laugh or cry.

"This is the worst kept secret ever," said Brittany.

"What secret," asked another new voice?

It was the happy voice of Maria. "I love secrets," she said, giggling.

"We're all going to escape," said Petrea, bluntly.

At Petrea's words Maria blinked twice and stopped laughing. Her face became pale and somber.

"I see," was all she could say in reply. The usual lightness was gone from her voice.

Cilantra took a deep breath.

"There are eight of us who know." began Cilantra. "That is too many to keep a secret for long."

She looked thoughtfully at each of the girls before continuing.

"We must not tell any of the others. Our lives are at stake."

The girls all nodded in agreement.

Lee'a took a step forward.

"The Prince will be very displeased if he learns of this," she said solemnly. "You have no idea what he would do."

Her eyes filled with tears and her bottom lip quivered as she spoke.

"He is a bad man; a very bad man."

As if her own words were too much for her to bear, Lee'a hid behind Armonia, again.

Suddenly, loud clapping came from the front of the shop; a signal from the Head Guard.

"We must go," declared Cilantra, "but not all together. Leave the shop in ones or twos."

With that Brittany and Cilantra disappeared beyond the loom.

In time, the eight girls managed to leave the shop without creating suspicion. They lined up in their usual order, with Cilantra and Brittany at the front.

The guards quickly brought the girls through the city gates and down the road toward the harbor. An unruly crowd formed along the road. It seemed the whole town wanted to offer the Favored Ones merchandise, trinkets and treats, for a price.

Items were thrust from the crowd toward the line of girls. Blin-Blin was dangled in front of their covered faces. Hands reached out to touch them. The guards did nothing to stop it.

As the road approached the docks, the sellers were replaced by working fishermen who barely glanced sideways at the Favored Ones The girls walked unhindered once again.

Cilantra could not take her eyes from the harbor. She scanned the moorings, docks and slips for any sign of *Emeraldsea.* Brittany and the others did likewise. If she were there, *Emeraldsea* would not go unnoticed.

The Head Guard clapped his hands and pointed to a rocky seawall built long out into the harbor. At the end was a tall stone signal tower.

The Head Guard droned on and on using the tower as an example of "the great achievements of Saalespor".

"It was light from this same tower that brought *The Black Claw* into safe harbor during the storm," intoned the Head Guard.

"If it were not for this tower," he proclaimed, "*The Black Claw* might have been lost, and you along with her."

"If it were not for *The Black Claw*," muttered Petrea, "we would be safe and happy at home."

"Even now," continued the Head Guard, "you can see men stacking new firewood at the top of the tower. It will again be ready in only one more day."

None of the girls listened to the lecture. They just walked on along the shore, scanning the sea for any sign of the *Emeraldsea*.

The farther they traveled from the city the closer the desert came to the beach. The desert sand was coarse and reddish-brown while the beach sand was fine and white.

A sharp turn in the coast forced the girls to scramble up a steep incline to a plateau. From here, the girls watched as waves crashed mightily against the rocky shore below.

On the downward side they could see a view of poignant beauty. Red desert sand collided with white beach sand and blue water.

Cilantra cried out loudly as she gazed down at the beach.

"Yes," proclaimed the Head Guard when he heard her gasp. "The precious sands of Saalespor; there's nothing like 'em."

The man smiled his cheeriest smile, which still was a bit scary.

Cilantra broke ranks and ran down the steep pathway toward the beach. A guard started after her, but was stopped by the grinning Head Guard.

"Let her go," order the Head Guard.

"I felt the same way the first time I saw this view."

In this, he seemed almost human.

Moments later, Brittany, Armonia, Petrea, Coral, Corree and Maria rushed down the same path toward the beach.

"I'll just go with them," declared Lee'a. She ran as fast as her little legs would take her.

As they reached the beach at the bottom of the cliff the girls found Cilantra kneeling in the shallow water, sobbing. Pieces of splintered hand-hewed planks floated around her; just so much flotsam.

The other girls walked silently among the debris that was scattered on the rocks and sand. Ropes and shredded sailcloth were strewn on the beach. A huge tree-like mast was partially buried in the sand and angled sharply into the air.

Brittany sloshed through the water to where her friend wept. As she too knelt in the surf she saw that Cilantra clutched a piece of wood to her chest. Brittany gently touched Cilantra's hands.

Cilantra looked at Brittany with eyes of the broken-hearted and slowly turned the plank toward her friend.

Brittany gasped aloud as she read the letters carved into the plank: *'Emeral'*. The plank was shattered after the letter "l".

CHAPTER 4
Day and Night

*I*t was past noon before Reed, the ninth brother in the House of Hiram, boarded *Vengeance.*

Quasar and Nemo watched from *Fyrmatus* as each ship came alongside *Vengeance* and sent one of the Lord Hiram's sons to her deck via a swing line.

One end of the swing line was tied to V*engeance's* main mast. The other end was thrown to whatever ship came alongside. The son would grab the line as high up as he could reach and throw himself into the air, braving the open sea between the ships.

If it worked correctly, the line would swing him over the *Vengeance's* deck and he would land there safely. If it didn't work correctly, the unfortunate son might be smashed into the side of ship, get caught in the rigging, or fall into the sea.

"This reminds me of a great complicated dance," said Nemo.

"What?" replied Quasar.

He was so engrossed watching Lord Reed swing from *Advocate* to *Vengeance* that he really wasn't listening to Nemo.

The crew aboard *Vengeance* had a hard time holding onto Reed once he came over. For some reason, Reed would not let go of the swing line. They grappled with him for what seemed to them like hours. It was really only seconds.

Finally, convinced that he would not fall into the sea, Reed let go of the swing line. He and the four men who caught him fell in a big heap on the deck of *Vengeance*.

"A great complicated dance," repeated Nemo. "A ship comes in and then bows out," he continued; "over and over again, like the moves of a dance."

Quasar looked at his best friend wondering if he had been hit in the head.

"It's not like any dance I've seen," he replied laughing. "Nor you, for that matter."

Nemo smiled and shook his head. He started to explain again about the dance, but thought better of it.

Advocate pulled away from *Vengeance*, as Reed tried to save his dignity. He stood among the four men who had caught him and smoothed his uniform as if nothing had happened. His four catchers quickly found somewhere else to be onboard the ship.

Quasar and Nemo watched as brothers Ram and Vine approached Reed patting him on the back and laughing heartily. They were closest in age to Reed and loved to tease him.

If Quasar and Nemo could have heard their conversation aboard *Vengeance* they might have heard something like:

"Ram, that swing line was your idea, wasn't it?" exclaimed Reed, hotly. It was more of an accusation than a question.

"Worked great!" replied Ram with a smile.

"Maybe for someone your size," said Reed, indignantly. "You're a head taller than me and as heavy as one of your war machines."

"It's good to see you too," laughed Ram. "And you're welcome."

"You should be thankful we didn't go along with his first idea," interjected Vine.

"Which was…?" replied Reed.

"A catapult," answered Ram, lightly. "I wanted to see if I could throw you up into the crow's nest." Ram laughed his deep barrel-chested laugh.

"I bet you did," replied Reed, joining in on the laughter.

"Come on," said Vine, smiling. "Everyone else is here. You don't want to keep Father waiting."

Quasar and Nemo watched as Lords Reed, Vine and Ram walked out of view.

The laughter ended as the three went below deck. At the bottom of the stairs stood two men wearing the white uniform of the Lord Hiram's elite personal guard.

Recognizing Lords Reed, Vine and Ram, the Service of Light, as they are called, let them pass without comment.

The three stopped before a great veil that separated the stairwell and hallway from the council room.

The veil was adorned with ten metal shields, one for each of the Lord Hiram's sons. Each shield was etched with the emblem of twin black hawks and colored according to each son's battle flag; sky blue for Herald, dark blue for

Norrom, orange for Tulmar, yellow for Shank, forest green for Reed, purple for Ram, and so on.

Kyler's silver shield was marked with a black stripe. Ram gently touched his late brother's shield, running his finger diagonally from top-left to right-bottom. He sighed deeply.

Like Reed and Vine, Ram removed his boots and stood, trying to compose himself. Then, taking deep breaths the three stepped through the veil and into the council room.

Ten huge, glistening silk sheets hung around the edges of the room. They were colored in the same colors as the ten shields. The banners stirred faintly as the three entered.

The center of the room held a large round table made of a handsome white wood. It was inlaid at the center with a shield of pure gold and etched with the image of twin black hawks.

Lords Reed, Vine and Ram took their places at the table. The nine brothers stood around the table in order of rank, each with their own colored banner for a backdrop. The chair before the silver banner remained empty.

Reed smiled when he saw his younger brother, Gannon, standing at the table. Gannon's many-colored striped banner hung proudly with the rest.

The Lord Hiram stood at the far end of the room, opposite the veil. His white hair hung almost to his shoulders. He was tall and powerfully built. He smiled warmly when his three sons entered. His teeth were perfectly white, but his eyes remained cold steel blue.

The Lord Hiram looked around at his sons.

"Please sit," he said simply; "Except you, Falcon. You, I will need here at my side."

The brothers looked cautiously at one another. No council, meeting, gathering or dinner had ever begun this way. Trying desperately not to be alarmed, the brothers sat without speaking.

Falcon moved with false ease toward his father. The two stood facing each other. Without ceremony, the Lord Hiram held out an elaborate sheath and belt. A shiver ran down Falcon's spine as he tied the belt around his waist.

"We are no longer just father and sons," said the Lord Hiram. His eyes moved from son to son around the table. "We are all men; we have all known battle and death."

His voice was heavy with sadness, but nonetheless, there was a special strength about it. His eyes shifted for a moment to the empty chair that would have been filled by his son, Kyler.

"I thought your brother's death at Three Rivers would usher in a time of peace. I comforted myself with that thought," said the Lord Hiram, quietly. "I was wrong," he said, his voice gaining in volume and intensity.

The Lord Hiram turned to his right. A huge double-edged broadsword hung on the wall near him. When it was in place it signified that the House of Hiram was at peace, when removed, it could only mean war.

Taking an immensely deep breath, the Lord Hiram grasped the hilt in his right hand and slowly lifted the heavy sword from its place of peace. Light seemed to spark from the sharp double-edged blade.

Suddenly, with one elegant motion, the Lord Hiram held the sword aloft and then, after a moment, brought it down in a quick and terrible slash. The sound of it slicing the air resounded in the room.

"Falcon, we are again at war," declared the Lord Hiram. "But, this is your war."

Falcon stood as tall as he could, eyes riveted upon his father and on the sword in his hand.

"An evil has struck at our hearts, but your heart, it has pierced."

The Lord Hiram turned to fully face his son.

"The House of Hiram will do all that we can to get Cilantra back," said the Lord Hiram firmly; "But this is your war."

With that, the Lord Hiram did the last thing any of his sons could have imagined. He handed Falcon the great battle sword.

Tulmar, Shank and Norrom shouted their approval. Ram and Vine pounded their fists on the table. Herald and Gannon clapped loudly. Only Reed sat still. A momentary shadow crossed his face and his heart, but he quickly recovered. He joined his brothers clapping, pounding and shouting loudest of all.

Near Falcon, standing in an ornate holder, was the Lord Hiram's mighty Golden Rod. Six feet long, the rod symbolized the authority and history of the House of Hiram. Made of gold-covered ironwood, the staff was engraved with scenes of important events. The birth and coronation of the Lord Hiram were represented, as was the birth of Falcon. The latest etching was the fiery death of Lord Kyler at the Battle of Three Rivers.

The Golden Rod was topped with a solid gold headpiece of twin hawks, looking in opposite directions. Wrapped around the base of the headpiece was a dying dragon.

The Lord Hiram stepped to the Golden Rod and removed it from its holder.

The brothers stopped their noise-making and reverently stood. All eyes were upon their father and his Golden Rod.

With slow deliberate movements the Lord Hiram raised the rod and slammed it against the floor. He did this three times. The blows echoed in the room and were felt throughout the ship.

The Lord Hiram handed the great Golden Rod to his oldest son and shouted, "Now, right this wrong, rescue your wife and honor the House of Hiram!"

Standing with sword in his right hand and rod in his left Falcon proclaimed loudly,

"I shall find Cilantra, the wife of my youth, and bring her home, and so it shall be for Brittany, as well."

At hearing this, a slight frown and quizzical expression came upon the Lord Hiram's face.

"Brittany, the bride of Quasar the Dragon-Slayer, was taken as well," explained Falcon, quickly.

The Lord Hiram nodded his head in understanding saying, "And so it shall be for Brittany, as well!"

The brothers pounded their fists on the table.

"Now sit, all," commanded the Lord Hiram as he took his seat.

"Falcon must tell us what he has learned of Cilantra and Brittany," said the Lord Hiram, "and we have much to tell him."

The men all sat, but Falcon remained standing. He put the sword into the sheath that hung from his belt and placed the Golden Rod back into its holder.

Falcon paced back and forth before speaking.

"I have learned that Cilantra and Brittany were kidnapped and taken aboard a wretched ship called *The Black Claw*," began Falcon. "They are prisoners in the palace of the Prince of Saalespor.

"How have you learned this?" asked Reed.

It was an honest question by one who deals with spies and lies on a daily basis.

"Quasar the Dragon-Slayer and Nemo Lord of Silverglade are aboard my ship," answered Falcon, a little formally. "They came with a man named Brock who…"

"Quasar and Nemo are here?" interrupted Gannon.

Quasar and Nemo were his first and best friends outside of the House of Hiram.

"Yes," answered Falcon smiling. "You'll see them soon enough."

The Lord Hiram rang a small bell that sat near his place at the table. He whispered to the man from the Service of Light who came in response to his call. The man left immediately.

"How did they come in the middle of the sea?" asked Norrom.

Always the Admiral, the fleet's security was one of his top concerns.

"They came on a lone sloop called *Emeraldsea*," said Falcon to Norrom. "We met by chance just as the storm hit."

"Who is this man, Brock?" asked Reed.

His spies had reported that Quasar and Nemo departed Mecenas aboard *Emeraldsea*, but they knew nothing about Brock.

"Brock is her captain, and friend of Quasar and Nemo," said Falcon to Reed. "What else do we need to know?"

Falcon locked eyes with Reed until the younger brother looked away.

"He is a fine sailor and a brave man," continued Falcon. "I trust him because they trust him."

Looking back to his brother, Reed smiled and slightly nodded his head.

"What about this prince?" asked the Lord Hiram. There was steel in his voice.

"Emeraldsea followed *The Black Claw* to the port of Saalespor," explained Falcon. "Brock made it to shore and even saw Cilantra and Brittany being led to the prince's palace."

The brothers all began shouting at the same time. Finally, the Lord Hiram raised his hand and the room became quiet. He motioned with his head for Falcon to continue.

"*Emeraldsea* found her way back to us while the seas were calm, but the storm hit again and we had to cut her loose."

"Is that all," asked the Lord Hiram?

Falcon shook his head and said, "No."

"The plan was for *Emeraldsea* to sail back to the harbor," answered Falcon. "She could enter the harbor with a lot less attention than *Fyrmatus*. Since she made it there once in a storm, we thought she could do it again."

Falcon's voice trailed off as he stared into a distant void.

"And…?" asked Gannon.

"Brock was to learn as much as he could and rescue them if possible," answered Falcon.

"One man?" asked Shank.

"We didn't think he could really rescue them by himself," said Falcon honestly, "but he could learn how, and when and where."

Falcon paused as the weakness of his plan struck his heart afresh.

"We were to rendezvous with *Emeraldsea* off the coast of Saalespor," said Falcon with downcast eyes.

The room became uncomfortably still. All eyes rested on Falcon. Taking a deep breath Falcon looked squarely at his father.

"We've been sailing off the coast of Saalespor for over two weeks," he confessed.

"But in the storm, we could see nothing. Today was the first decent day we've had."

"You're a fine sailor," said Norrom, breaking through the gloom that had descended upon the room.

"Most would have run aground in that storm."

"And now the storm is over," added Shank, eagerly.

"We'll find *Emeraldsea,*" declared Tulmar, loudly.

"We'll find Cilantra," shouted Ram and Vine together.

"We have much to discuss," declared the Lord Hiram.

At that, Falcon joined his brothers sitting at the table. Reed told Falcon all that his spies had uncovered. Norrom spoke of the preparations the fleet had made. Each of the brothers was eager to tell his part. Only Gannon did not speak, but his eyes twinkled with a deeply held secret.

Finally, the Lord Hiram leaned forward at the table. His steel blue eyes became hard and cold as he described his plans for Prince Rhala'nn and the miserable kingdom of Saalespor.

"I know she is your wife, and so this fight is yours to lead," said the Lord Hiram, sitting back in his chair. "But Cilantra is also a member of the House of Hiram and mother to my grandchildren." A fire ignited behind his eyes as the Lord Hiram spoke.

"We will rescue Cilantra," said the Lord Hiram, firmly.

"And Brittany," added Gannon, without thinking.

The Lord Hiram stared at his youngest son for a moment, and then smiled.

"And Brittany," he added.

"Then, we will teach this Prince Rhala'nn to regret his wickedness."

The Lord Hiram paused and looked directly at Gannon.

"The precious sands of Saalespor will never be the same," he said with fire in his eyes.

Before Gannon or anyone else could speak, a member of the Service of Light entered the room and nodded to the Lord Hiram.

"Tea and sweet cakes have been prepared on deck. Go and refresh yourselves," said the Lord Hiram. He spoke now as a kind father. The voice of the fearsome warrior was gone.

"Tea?" asked Reed in wonder.

"Ah, sweet cakes," exclaimed Ram, who was always hungry.

"Falcon and I will stay here and discuss a few details," said the Lord Hiram, standing.

In response, all the sons of the Lord Hiram stood in unison. The meeting was over.

"Go," said the Lord Hiram, with a twinkle in his eye. "It would be impolite to keep our guests waiting."

"Guests?" asked Gannon.

"Quasar and Nemo, of course," answered the Lord Hiram.

Gannon almost tripped over his chair as he rushed from the table. The metal shields on the veil clattered as he ran through. He even startled the guards from the Service of Light at the foot of the stairs, and that is hard to do.

A table had been brought on deck near the galley. It was set with steaming pots of tea, mugs, and a platter of sweet cakes. Quasar and Nemo stood staring out at sea. Gannon rushed up behind them from below deck, calling their names.

Quasar turned wearing a great smile. Nemo turned too, wiping crumbs from his lips.

"I told you we should wait," whispered Quasar.

"I only ate one," replied Nemo through his frozen smile.

The reunion was loud and happy as Gannon and his brothers greeted their guests with hugs and pats on the back.

Everyone talked at the same time, between slurping mugs and mouths full of sweet cake. In all the laughter and excitement, Nemo still managed to eat three more sweet cakes.

Signal flags were hoisted and ships came, one at a time, alongside *Vengeance*.

"It is good to see you," shouted Norrom with a wave. "I look forward to meeting your friend Brock," he added as he jumped into the air.

Holding a swing line from his ship *Sea Core*, Norrom was the first to rejoin his own ship. Soon all the others were doing likewise. In and out came the ships in perfect harmony.

Quasar, Nemo and Gannon watched, each engrossed in his own thoughts.

"It's like the moves of a great complicated dance," said Nemo, breaking the silence.

"I know exactly what you mean," replied Gannon.

Quasar stared at his two friends.

"Are you kidding me?" he muttered.

"What?" exclaimed Nemo and Gannon.

Changing the subject, Quasar pointed toward the horizon.

"Is that your ship?" he asked.

"Yes," replied Gannon. "She's called *Scorpion*," he added. There was a touch of pride in his voice.

"Why is she so far out," asked Nemo? "The other ships sail together as a fleet, but she stays out there, on the horizon."

"*Scorpion* has a very special passenger," answered Gannon, with a smile. "Besides, *Vengeance* provides us escort."

"If the passenger is so special, wouldn't it be better for the whole fleet to be close so she could be protected," asked Nemo?

"*Scorpion* is so far away, the fleet offers no protection at all," added Quasar.

"The passenger doesn't need protection by the fleet," said Gannon, mysteriously. "The fleet needs protection from the passenger," said Gannon with an odd grin.

"You're protecting the fleet from your passenger?" asked Quasar.

"That's why *Scorpion* sails so far from the fleet," said Gannon plainly.

Quasar looked intently at *Scorpion*.

Nemo looked blankly at Gannon.

"I don't understand," they both admitted.

"Alright," said Gannon seriously. "Look up."

Quasar and Nemo both looked up into the sails and rigging of the ship.

"No," laughed Gannon. "Look up above *Scorpion*."

They turned and gazed out to sea toward *Scorpion*.

"Do you see anything?" asked Gannon.

Nemo shook his head, but Quasar just kept watching the ship.

"Look above her riggings, said Gannon. "Do you see anything at all?" he asked again.

Nemo and Quasar kept staring at *Scorpion*. They both just shook their heads.

"I see your battle flag," said Nemo.

Gannon smiled and shook his head.

Finally, Quasar pointed to something that could barely be seen from the deck of *Vengeance*.

"What's that?" he asked, slowly.

He was not even sure he could really see anything at all.

"*Scorpion* has a very special passenger," answered Gannon. His smile was replaced by an extremely serious expression.

Suddenly, Quasar took a backward step.

"That's not possible!" he exclaimed.

"Yes, it is," replied Gannon with a knowing smile.

Nemo looked at Quasar, then Gannon, then *Scorpion* and then back at Quasar.

"What's not possible?" he asked.

"How did you…?" Quasar asked.

Gannon just kept smiling.

"How did he what?" asked Nemo.

"How, how, why…?" stammered Quasar.

"How can he what?" demanded Nemo. "Why would who," he added? "What are you two talking about!" shouted Nemo.

ೞ   ೞ   ೞ   ೞ   ೞ

Cilantra slowly looked around, blinking, unable to remember where she was or how she got there. In her hands she held a large skein of red silk cord. Setting it on the ground, she realized she was sitting on a bench in a garden. As the fog retreated from her mind, she realized she had not been asleep, but it seemed as if she were just now waking.

"Oh, I'm so glad you're back," said a familiar voice. "You really had me worried."

"Brittany!" cried Cilantra. "Where are we, what has happened?" Cilantra's voice was filled with panic.

"We're in the Woman's Garden, in the palace," replied Brittany. "The others have gone to their rooms. I told them we wanted to rest here after the long walk."

Cilantra looked around the garden. Her face was blank.

"What do you remember?" asked Brittany. The hope in her voice was changing to worry. She stood as they talked.

"Nothing makes sense," said Cilantra in a quivering voice. Tears began to flow down her cheeks.

"What palace?" she managed to ask.

"Just try to relax," suggested Brittany.

The fog slowly lifted from Cilantra. Suddenly, horribly, dark memories rushed back;

the kidnapping, *The Black Claw*, the palace, the garden, the guards, the city and the sea.

"*Emeraldsea!*" she screamed.

Brittany quickly sat next to Cilantra wrapping loving arms around her.

Cilantra rocked back and forth weeping at the horror of it all. Memories flooded her mind in a disconnected jumble of scenes.

The two stayed on the bench, consoling one another, until sunset. Something about the cool of the evening and the night sounds of insects and frogs brought a muted peace to the girls.

"How did I get back here?" asked Cilantra. Her voice told Brittany that she was becoming herself again.

"Do you remember this?" ask Brittany, cautiously. In her hand she held a wooden plank that she had hidden behind the bench. On it was carved '*Emeral*'.

Cilantra nodded silently as she ran her fingers over the letters that partially spelled *Emeraldsea*. She remembered it. She remembered everything.

Cilantra took the plank into her own hands and hugged it tightly to her chest.

Sighing, she asked, "How did I get back here?"

"It was Lee'a," answered Brittany. "Somehow she got the guards to allow us to travel back in little groups rather than in guarded lines." Brittany smiled as she told the story.

"You were in a daze," continued Brittany. "Armonia held one of your arms and I the other," Brittany said quietly.

"Petrea walked directly in front of you, like some kind of shield." Brittany paused, not wanting to overwhelm Cilantra. "Petrea was tremendous."

Brittany stopped talking. Remembering the events of the day brought up a wellspring of emotion she had not expected. After a few minutes, however, she regained her composure. Breathing deeply, she began again.

"Eventually, we got back to the city and from there the palace. We had to walk in two lines once we entered the city gates."

Details flooded Brittany's mind. She struggled with what she should and should not tell Cilantra.

"What's this?" asked Cilantra. She held up the skein of red silk cord.

"It's nothing," answered Brittany, casually.

"The guard insisted that we all bring back something to remember our tour. He brought us to the shop we had visited in the morning."

Brittany smiled slyly before continuing.

"I think the Head Guard's family owns the shop." She shook her head and smiled coyly. "Anyway, he insisted we each choose something, and paid for it all."

"But, what is this?" repeated Cilantra.

"When we entered the shop it was like you were sleeping with your eyes open." replied Brittany. "You wouldn't talk or respond to anything."

Cilantra didn't think this answered her question, but feeling still confused, she said nothing.

"We sat you down on a chair in the back corner of the shop, near the loom, where you would be safe."

Cilantra nodded her head and smiled, but she still didn't understand.

"Before we knew it, the Head Guard clapped his hands and it was time to leave," explained Brittany. Her words became quick and filled with tension.

"You didn't choose anything to buy, so I grabbed something, anything, from the shelf near your chair."

Cilantra looked at the skein of red silk cord. She turned it in her hand, examining all sides, rubbing her fingers over the cord.

"You chose this as my souvenir?" asked Cilantra, with a smile in her voice.

"I've never been good at shopping," Brittany answered, with a chuckle.

Both girls started laughing. The fear and tension of the day melted away. In time, Brittany nodded toward dark forms moving about in the garden.

"I think we need to get back to our rooms," she said quietly. "The night guards are beginning to patrol."

"You're right," said Cilantra, "but first, I want to thank you."

She gave Brittany a big hug.

Brittany and Cilantra moved quickly to the stairway that went up to their rooms. They quietly made their way up the stairs and down the hallway. When they arrived at the door to Cilantra's rooms, she shyly looked down.

"Brittany, would you mind very much if I stayed in your room tonight?" asked Cilantra.

"I would love it," answer Brittany. "I don't want to be alone, either. It's been a hard day."

Arm in arm the girls walked down the hall and entered Brittany's room. It was dark, except for an oil lamp burning on the terrace.

They lit several more lamps. Warm light bathed the room and lifted their spirits.

"I'm hungry," announced Cilantra as she passed a fresh dinner tray on the terrace. She took a dried fig from the tray and popped it into her mouth.

"I bet Lee'a left a tray in your room, too," replied Brittany.

"Let's go get it and we can eat together," said Cilantra.

Happily, Cilantra opened the door between their rooms and walked into her suite. Brittany walked behind her.

Suddenly, Cilantra froze. She stopped so quickly that Brittany bumped into her.

"Hey," squealed Brittany, playfully.

"Shhh," whispered Cilantra. "Something's wrong."

"What do you mean?" asked Brittany.

She was sure Cilantra was still a bit dazed.

"The lamp on the terrace isn't lit," answered Cilantra. "Lee'a always lights it."

"Maybe the wind blew it out," said Brittany.

She quickly retrieved a lamp from her room and returned to the connecting doorway. Holding the lamp high, she said, "Let's take a look."

Slowly, the two girls moved into the darkened suite. Brittany's lamp cast a ring of light around them as they moved.

Cilantra stopped moving.

"Someone's been here," she said quietly. Her voice was strong and sure.

"How do you know?" asked Brittany. She was beginning to feel frightened.

"I can smell them, sweaty and salty, like the ocean, answered Cilantra.

"Maybe we should call Kuubow," said Brittany. She was really feeling frightened, now.

"No, just light more lamps," said Cilantra. Her voice was cautious, but not fearful.

Together they walk around the room, lighting lamps wherever they could be found.

Brittany moved to light the lamp on the terrace. What she found there almost caused her to scream.

"The food tray is here," said Brittany. Her voice quivered. "But the food has been eaten."

Light from the lamp revealed a dinner tray with much of the food spilled about, as if it had been eaten in haste.

Expecting some comment from Cilantra, but getting none, Brittany slowly turned back to face the room. Cilantra was gone.

A shiver ran down Brittany's back.

"Cilantra?" called Brittany, quietly.

No answer.

"Cilantra?" she called again, louder; still, no answer.

Brittany noticed light coming from the bedroom.

"Cilantra, are you ok?" asked Brittany.

She started to move toward the bedroom, but stopped when she heard Cilantra's answer.

"He's here."

ぺ　ぺ　ぺ　ぺ　ぺ

"What is it now?" roared Prince Rhala'nn.

Fezala, his personal aide, stood patiently, waiting for the tantrum to subside.

"How dare you awaken me at this hour," screamed the prince.

"Forgive me, Lord," replied Fezala, "but you summoned me, did you not?"

Prince Rhala'nn sat on the side of his massive bed, holding his head in his hands.

He said nothing in reply to Fezala's cautious question.

"How may I be of service?" asked Fezala, carefully, quietly. If the prince had fallen asleep while sitting up, Fezala did NOT want to awaken him.

Finally, Rhala'nn lifted his head.

"What time is it?" he asked.

To Fezala, it seemed the prince was ready to rage regardless of his answer.

"It is not yet 10 by the clock, my Lord," answered Fezala, carefully. "I gave you your sleeping tonic not a half hour ago. Perhaps you dozed off."

Prince Rhala'nn stood and walked sleepily to a window. Looking out, he could see nothing unusual in the courtyard below.

"What was all the noise? he asked.

"Noise?" asked Fezala.

He had hoped the prince would sleep through the events of the night and did not want to be the one to inform him of them.

"I heard the sound of voices, horses, armor," declared the prince. "It woke me."

"My apologies, Lord," said Fezala, coolly. "Allow me to get you another sleeping tonic."

"If I wanted a sleeping tonic I would order a sleeping tonic," hissed the prince.

"Of course," said Fezala, taking a backward step and bowing deeply.

"I want answers!" screamed the prince.

"Very well, Lord. I will summon your counselors," said Fezala, in an oily reply.

He hoped, in this way, to leave the room with his head intact and bring others to deliver the bad news.

Prince Rhala'nn's eyes narrowed dangerously as he looked at his aide.

"I want answers from you," he said menacingly, emphasizing the word 'you'. "What are you hiding from me?"

Fezala knew this was not a good sign. *How can I answer him without killing myself*, he thought?

"Are we under attack?" asked Rhala'nn. "You would tell me if we were under attack, wouldn't you?"

"You would be the first to know, my Lord," answered Fezala. He smiled reassuringly.

"Then what is it? What was all the noise?" Rhala'nn looked fiercely at Fezala. "Tell me, now," ordered the prince.

"It was just your personal guard," answered Fezala. He tried with all his skill to sound casual and confident even though he was neither.

"What about my guard?" asked Rhala'nn. He moved unsteadily back to the bed.

"They went on maneuvers, sir," answered Fezala, truthfully enough.

"At night?" shrieked Rhala'nn. "I did not order them on maneuvers!"

"No sir, you did not," was the only thing Fezala could think to say.

"Then who did?" hissed the prince.

Fezala had been Rhala'nn's personal aide longer than any of the others before him. He feared his time might be quickly coming to an end.

"The King did, my Lord," answered Fezala in a practiced voice.

"My father?" bellowed Rhala'nn.

"General Ryguy Roces came personally this very night, with orders from the King," said Fezala in reply.

"What orders?" thundered the prince. "Answer truthfully, or you will pay with pain!"

The prince took a step toward Fezala. "You will beg me to kill you when I am through, if you lie," warned Rhala'nn.

"My life is to serve," professed Fezala, bowing toward Rhala'nn.

Fezala swallowed hard. *So this is the day I die*, he thought to himself.

Choosing his words with care, Fezala answered the prince.

"The King ordered, that is requested, three-fourths of your personal guard to his palace, fully armed and on horseback. They left with General Ryguy Roces less than an hour ago." Fezala was careful to speak only the truth.

When Rhala'nn said nothing Fezala continued.

"I was coming to tell you when you summoned me," said Fezala, carefully. It was a lie.

"What does my father want with my personal guard?" asked Rhala'nn. "What is he planning?"

"Forgive me, my Lord,' replied Fezala, dryly. "The King rarely discusses his plans with me."

Rhala'nn looked at him with a puzzled expression. Fortunately for Fezala, Rhala'nn didn't recognize the sarcasm.

"Of course he doesn't," barked Rhala'nn.

"Exactly, my Lord," intoned Fezala, as if the prince had come to some monumental insight.

"If you learn anything… come… tell…" began the prince as he lay down on his bed. He didn't finish his sentence.

"You will be the first to know, my Lord," promised Fezala.

After a few minutes of silence, Fezala quietly asked, "Shall I bring you a sleeping tonic, my Lord?"

The snoring of Prince Rhala'nn was his answer.

CB CB CB CB CB

Brittany was unsure what she should do.

She lit another oil lamp as she moved toward the bedroom.

"What did you say?" she asked, lightly.

Try as she might she could not make her voice sound calm. Looking around the room, she picked up a heavy vase to use as a weapon.

"He's here," repeated Cilantra. Her voice had a strange far away sound to it.

Brittany silently put the vase back on the table and picked up an even larger one. With an oil lamp in one hand and a big vase in the other she took another step toward the bedroom.

"Who's here, exactly?" she asked.

Brittany walked noiselessly toward the bedroom, stopping just before the open door.

"Brittany," came Cilantra's impatient voice. "What are you waiting for?" she asked. "Please, come here; hurry!"

Brittany took a deep breath and peeked quickly into the room. If anything was wrong, she planned to throw the vase and run screaming from the room.

She found Cilantra standing with her back to the doorway, facing the bed and holding a lamp in one hand. No one else was in the room.

"Cilantra, are you alright?" asked Brittany. She put the heavy vase back down.

"He's here," repeated Cilantra, emphatically. "Falcon is here!"

As she spoke, Cilantra stepped aside, revealing her bed and the things that lay on top of it.

Brittany could not make sense of what she saw.

Cilantra trembled so badly, the light from her lamp flickered and danced on the wall. Brittany gently took the lamp from her.

With a lamp in each hand, Brittany moved close to the bed and held the lamps high. Light shone brightly on the silky white bedcover.

"What does all this mean?" she whispered.

On the bed was a red leather cap emblazoned with Twin Black Hawks on a field of gold. Next to the cap was a single red flower and next to that was a small branch covered with large thorns.

Brittany and Cilantra silently stared at the items on the bed for what seem like a lifetime. Thoughts and questions swirled in their minds.

In time, Cilantra gently picked up the flower. Holding it to her nose, she breathed deeply of its sweet fragrance.

Brittany finally found her tongue.

"What does all this mean?" she asked, softly.

Cilantra looked Brittany full-faced.

"You know where the cap came from, don't you?" Cilantra asked.

"It's from Falcon, or one of his men," answered Brittany.

Cilantra nodded.

"You know my name," she continued, then paused to drink in the flower's fragrance once again.

"Of course I know your name," answered Brittany, dryly.

"In the old tongue, 'Cilantra' means 'sweet fragrant flower,'" said Cilantra.

She waved the flower slightly.

"Oh, I see," said Brittany.

"What about this," she asked?

As she spoke, Brittany reached to pick up the thorny branch.

"Stop!" shouted Cilantra.

Brittany jerked back her hand.

"What?" shouted Brittany in shock.

"Those thorns are deadly," explained Cilantra. "Don't touch them."

Brittany looked at the thorns, at Cilantra and then back at the thorns.

"I won't," she promised.

"They are called 'three-step' thorns," continued Cilantra. "Their poison is so strong that once you're pricked, you can only take three steps before you die."

Brittany subconsciously rubbed her fingers together and silently gave thanks she had not touched the thorns.

Taking a step away from the bed, Brittany asked again: "What does all this mean?"

"There is another word, much like 'Cilantra'. It is Celantra, with an 'e'". In the old tongue it means 'deadly thorn."

"I don't understand," said Brittany, humbly.

"There is a ship in the Lord Hiram's fleet that was named after me," explained Cilantra.

"Oh I see,' said Brittany; but she didn't really.

"Before it was launched, Admiral Norrom, Falcon's brother, suggested that a warship should not be named 'sweet fragrant flower.'"

"I can see his point," smiled Brittany. This much she understood.

"When it was launched, we christened the ship, *Celantra*," explained Cilantra, "instead of *Cilantra*."

"'Deadly thorn', instead of 'sweet fragrant flower.'" exclaimed Brittany.

"Yes."

"What does all this mean?" Brittany asked for the fourth time.

"Well, I can't be sure exactly, but it is a message from Falcon." Cilantra stopped talking and tried to make sense of it all.

"I think help is near," said Brittany, answering her own question. "Maybe a whole ship full of the Reds has landed."

Brittany smiled at the thought of being rescued by hundreds of the Lord Falcon's best troops. In her mind, Quasar would be with them.

"I'm not sure what it means," said Cilantra. "But I know one thing. It's a lot better news than when we saw *Emeraldsea* on the beach."

"That's for sure," said Brittany.

Yawning, she was suddenly very, very tired.

"We need to be ready for anything," declared Cilantra.

"What do we need to do?" asked Brittany.

"I think you should sleep in here," suggested Cilantra. "If they come back, we may have only moments to escape with them."

"Good idea,' said Brittany. "I didn't really want to be all by myself tonight, anyway," she said lightheartedly.

In a more serious tone, she asked, "Do you really think they might come back tonight?"

CHAPTER 5
Morning Bright

*B*right morning light danced upon Brittany's face; glare and shadow performing a pas de duex above her eyes. Squinting painfully, she moaned and pulled the covers over her head.

Her face reappeared as she looked sleepily around the room. After a moment, she remembered where she was and what had happened. She quietly slipped out of bed.

On the bed stand was the red flower in a small bowl of water. Its sweet fragrance filled the room. The stick of poisonous thorns and the red cap from last night's visitor were nowhere to be seen.

A sudden noise on the terrace startled Brittany. She quickly put on her slippers and robe and started to make her way out of the bedroom.

STOP, shouted her mind!

Brittany halted just before the open bedroom door.

How do you know Cilantra is out there, her mind asked?

Who else would it be, she answered herself?

Maybe it's the visitor from last night, cautioned her mind?

Fear is a poor leader, but caution is the way of the wise, she reminded herself.

It was one of Quasar's favorite sayings.

Brittany closed her eyes, lowered her head to concentrate and listened carefully. She could hear no one talking or any noise whatsoever through the open doorway. Taking a deep breath, she prepared to peek around the door.

"What are you doing?" came the cheerful voice of Cilantra.

It startled Brittany so much that she gasped as her eyes flew open. Cilantra was standing inches away on the other side of the open doorway.

"Listening," said Brittany, blushing. She was now fully awake, eyes wide and a little shaky.

"Oh," replied Cilantra, simply. "I'm glad to see you're awake; breakfast?"

Cilantra turned and casually walked toward the terrace. Brittany followed, but could not help looking around the room to make sure someone was not lurking there.

"I tidied up the dinner tray from last night," said Cilantra as they entered the terrace. "It seems our visitor has the manners of a Porco or was in a big hurry."

"I never thought of that," said Brittany, looking around again for a hidden foe. "Do you think it was a Porco?" asked Brittany, alarm rising in her heart.

"I don't think a Porco would leave flowers," replied Cilantra, lightly. "And, we would have smelled him."

"Right," agreed Brittany, laughing a little. "Or caps," she added. "Where is the red cap?" Brittany wondered aloud.

"I hid it in the bed stand drawer." answered Cilantra. "I don't want Lee'a asking questions."

"Good idea," said Brittany. "She looks young, but there is something old about her. I am never sure what she is thinking."

"I got the dinner tray from your room," said Cilantra. "When Lee'a brings breakfast I want it to look like we ate together last night."

Brittany nodded. "That's a good idea, too" she said.

"We don't want her, or anyone else, to suspect he was here," explained Cilantra.

Most of the dinner was unattractive at this point, but the girls shared a few orange slices and some dry flat bread.

"How long have you been up?" asked Brittany. She noticed a pile of red silk cord in the far corner of the terrace.

"It looks like you've been busy," she said, pointing to the pile.

"I've been braiding the cord you bought me into a rope," said Cilantra. "I have a plan," she added with a smile.

The sharp sound of tinkling bells stopped Cilantra cold. She glanced at the door that opens to the outside hallway.

"Quick", exclaimed Cilantra. "Help me bring the trays inside. I don't want them on the terrace. I don't want Lee'a seeing my rope."

ༀ   ༀ   ༀ   ༀ   ༀ

"Why did you wake me," shouted Prince Rhala'nn? "Why is it so bright," he screamed, pulling the covers over his face?

Fezala had barely opened the drapes when the prince started shrieking. He opened them even wider before answering.

"This is what it's like in the morning," said Fezala, dryly. "Something you rarely see, my Lord."

"You will pay with pain," came Rhala'nn's voice from under the covers.

"General Ryguy Roces is here to see you, my Lord," replied Fezala, hoping to change the subject.

"Well, I don't want to see him," answered the prince, angrily.

"Actually, my Lord, it is your father who wants to see you. The general is here to bring you to him," explained Fezala.

"What?" asked Rhala'nn in a voice that was wary and confused.

His sleep-crusted, squinty eyes peeked out from under the covers.

"The general will be here in a few moments, my Lord," said Fezala in a calm voice.

"Would you like to dress or go with him as you are?"

Fezala was clearly enjoying himself.

As he spoke, the sound of heavy boots echoed in the hallway that led to the prince's rooms.

Prince Rhala'nn's eyes widened in a panicked and surprised rage.

"Tell him I am dressing," bellowed the prince.

"As you wish, my Lord," replied Fezala.

He lowered his eyes and walked backwards from the room.

"My life is to serve."

His voice was as greasy as it was insincere.

ଔ   ଔ   ଔ   ଔ   ଔ

Falcon stood on the quarterdeck of *Fyrmatus* in full uniform. The great battle sword of the House of Hiram hung from his waist. He surveyed the fleet with satisfaction. Turning his gaze toward land, he could clearly see the shores of Saalespor. The fleet was deployed all along the coast.

Quasar and Nemo stood on the quarterdeck away from Falcon. They kept watch on the horizon, where *Vengeance* and *Scorpion* sailed, but said nothing.

Shaking his head, Quasar finally broke the silence.

"That is the most amazing thing I have ever heard," he said. His voice was filled with awe and disbelief.

"That is the most amazing thing I have ever seen," agreed Nemo. "At least I think I can see it."

Suddenly, a voice came from behind them.

"The Lord Falcon would like you to join him."

Quasar and Nemo both jumped at the sound and sight of Mr. Schooper. Without a word, they followed him to Falcon.

Falcon said nothing at first, so they just starred at the shore. Finally, he looked squarely at Quasar.

"This wretched pile of sand has imprisoned our wives long enough," said Falcon, anger smoldering in his voice. "I'm afraid we will put them in greater danger before we bring them safely home."

Without giving Quasar time to reply, Falcon pointed to the shore.

"Do you know what that is?" he asked.

Quasar and Nemo look at the shore where debris marred the sand and flotsam blemished the waves.

Nemo spotted a mast growing tree-like from the sand. It was angled sharply into the air.

"Oh no," cried Nemo.

"*Emeraldsea*," said Quasar, his voice surprised and discouraged.

"How well do you know Brock?" asked Falcon.

"What?" replied Nemo.

"Your friend, Brock; could he have survived this?" asked Falcon, directly. "How well do you know him?"

Quasar and Nemo looked at one another and then back at Falcon.

"We just met him," said Nemo, simply.

"We met him just a little before we sailed after *The Black Claw*," added Quasar.

"I told my father he was your friend," said Falcon, disappointment ringing in his voice.

"He is," said Nemo, confidently.

"He's a new friend," added Quasar, smiling weakly.

Falcon turned his gaze back to the wreckage of *Emeraldsea*.

"Could he have survived a shipwreck?" asked Falcon.

"Yes," said Quasar and Nemo with confidence.

"As well as any man," said Quasar.

"Better than most," added Nemo.

"He's fortunate to have friends like you," said Falcon with as much of a smile as he could manage. "Very fortunate; as am I."

ဢ ဢ ဢ ဢ ဢ

"This is Teal and this is Amber," said Lee'a sweetly. She gestured toward twin girls who had entered the room with her. They both held breakfast trays.

Teal and Amber looked exactly alike. They both had long fiery red hair and piercing emerald green eyes. In private, Teal was quiet and a little reserved whereas Amber smiled and laughed easily. Here, they both just stood wide-eyed waiting for someone to tell them what to do with the breakfast trays.

Cilantra and Brittany stared mutely at the two girls.

These two do not look like any Porco I have ever seen, thought Cilantra. *I wonder if they were kidnapped, too. They're so young!*

"I told them all about yesterday," said Lee'a, smiling. "They wanted to meet you."

"What exactly did you tell them about yesterday?" asked Cilantra, smiling.

Her words seemed offhanded, her voice disinterested. Nothing could be further from the truth.

Teal and Amber put down their trays on a table in the sitting room right next to the dinner trays Cilantra and Brittany had deposited just moments before.

Amber noticed that tea in a mug was still moving back and forth like ripples in a pond. She said nothing, but joined Teal in fluffing pillows and straightening things around the suite.

"May I serve you breakfast?" asked Lee'a.

"Oh, you needn't bother," said Cilantra, amiably. "We can do that, thanks."

She really just wanted Lee'a to leave, and with her the two others.

"Well, at least I can pour your tea," insisted Lee'a.

Not waiting for a reply, she picked up the teapot and poured its hot contents into two fresh mugs. Fragrance and steam swirled up from the tray. Brittany breathed it in gladly.

"What are you making?"

The voice came from either Teal or Amber; Cilantra wasn't sure. They were both standing on the terrace. Teal was holding a long braid of red silk rope. It flowed from her hands into a twisted pile at her feet.

Brittany gasped slightly when she saw them. Cilantra continued to smile sweetly, but starred wide-eyed in surprise. After blinking two or three times, she answered with the truth, of sorts.

"It's a surprise," she whispered. "You must not tell anyone."

Teal, Amber and Lee'a all nodded in agreement. The twins giggled as they put the rope back where they had found it.

"What kind of surprise," asked Lee'a?
She loved surprises.

Cilantra held a finger to her lips. "Shhhhhh," she said. "You must not tell anyone."

Lee'a nodded earnestly.

Teal and Amber picked up the dinner trays and followed Lee'a out the door. Just before the door closed, her head popped back inside.

"I won't tell anyone," Lee'a promised. With a wink and a smile she was gone.

ଔ ଔ ଔ ଔ ଔ

A lone man bent forward and pushed mightily against the handles of his cart, desperate to get it out of the way.

The pounding hoofs of war horses gave him just enough warning to move his fish cart to relative safety on the side of the road. He stopped near large iron gates that hung between two tall buildings. Behind the gates was a little guard shack. At the sound of the approaching horses two guards scrambled out of the shack.

The fish monger kept his head down as the horsemen rode by, but his eyes missed nothing. He saw someone of great import, like a prince, being escorted by someone of great power, like a general.

He saw, in fact, a very unhappy Prince Rhala'nn being escorted by the very powerful General Ryguy Roces.

Besides the early morning hour, which Rhala'nn found to be unbearable, he was especially unhappy to learn that his personal guard had been reduced overnight to a mere handful.

The truth was many of the men who rode with the general this morning had, until last night, been the prince's personal guard. They now wore the King's crest and flew the King's colors from the tips of their lances.

As the dust settled, one of the men from the guard shack came up to the iron gates and shouted at the fish monger.

"You there, you – get yur stink'n fish away from here."

The guard took a step back as the man stood up tall and moved toward him instead of retreating. His face held no fear, his hands and arms were strong, and his eyes were unflinching.

"Yur no Porco," said the guard. He had rarely seen an outsider.

"I'm no fish seller, either," answered the man.

The guard looked at the cart full of fresh fish. "What about that?" he asked.

"I'm here as a favor for a friend," answered the man.

The fact that the friend was Quasar and the favor was rescuing Brittany didn't come up in the conversation.

Brock reached into his jacket and pulled out a small paper-wrapped packet. Without warning, he tossed it to the guard.

"You look hungry," said Brock, in a friendly voice.

The guard caught and opened the packet to find a handful of sweet dates.

"These look good enough to eat," said the guard popping one of the dates into his mouth.

"What's going on here?" said the other guard when he heard the word 'eat'.

Brock quickly retrieved an orange from the cart and tossed it over the gate to the second guard.

"Well, I've got to go," said Brock. He returned to the cart and pretended to push it forward.

"I've got to get this fish delivered to the Prince's kitchen before it gets too hot."

"Well where do you think yur going?" asked the guard who had just caught the orange.

"Like I said," repeated Brock, "I've got to get this fish delivered to the Prince's kitchen."

"You can't push a fish cart up to the grand entrance of the palace," said the man laughing.

"No?" replied Brock, innocently.

"He don't know nothing," said one guard to the other.

"Come on through," said the first guard, unlocking and opening the gate.

"This will take you to the side entrance of the palace," he explained. "The first opening leads to the Woman's Garden. The one after that leads to the kitchen."

"Don't you go gett'n yourself into the Woman's Garden," said the other guard.

"Or you'll pay with pain for sure," laughed both the guards.

"Thank you," said Brock as he pushed the cart through the big iron gates. "Like I said, I'm here as a favor for a friend."

 CS   CS   CS   CS   CS

The knock on the door was quiet, but insistent. Brittany and Cilantra looked at one another in alarm.

"How are we going to explain our clothes?" asked Brittany.

"We don't explain anything," replied Cilantra. Her voice was filled with self-assurance.

"But, we're in hiking clothes," said Brittany; "not palace silks."

"There's no law against us wearing hiking clothes instead of palace clothes," said Cilantra, confidently.

"How do you know?" snapped Brittany. Her voice was edged in fear. "There might be."

Cilantra looked surprised at the thought, but said nothing. She walked boldly to the door and opened it.

Brittany and Cilantra were surprised to find Teal and Amber standing in the hallway, each holding part of a large sack.

"Teal and Amber," said Cilantra smoothly. "What a pleasant surprise."

Or is it Amber and Teal, thought Cilantra? *I can't tell them apart.*

The twins smiled and took a step into Cilantra's suite. Teal stepped in with her right foot, Amber with her left.

Reaching their hands forward, Teal (or perhaps it was Amber) said,

"Lee'a wants you to have this."

When neither Cilantra nor Brittany moved to take the sack, Teal and Amber set it on the floor and took a step backward.

"She said it's for your surprise," said Amber with a broad smile (or was it Teal?).

Brittany looked at the sack, blinked, and then looked mutely at the twins.

Cilantra was able to mask her surprise and said sweetly. "Please thank Lee'a for us. It's so thoughtful of her."

She stepped forward and placed her hand on the door. The two girls nodded in perfect unison as they moved back into the hallway.

"Bye," they both said, sweetly.

"Goodbye, and thank you so much," replied Cilantra as she shut the door.

"What do we do now?" asked Brittany, as soon as the door was fully shut.

"There's only one thing to do," answered Cilantra with a smile in her voice.

"What?" asked Brittany.

"Open the sack, of course," laughed Cilantra.

CȜ   CȜ   CȜ   CȜ   CȜ

Brock pushed the cart down the deserted alley. *That was just too easy*, he thought to himself.

He looked up and down the tall buildings that bordered the dark, dirty little alleyway.

No windows. No balconies. And no one to watch me come or go, thought Brock happily.

Ahead, Brock spied an opening in the alley. Through the opening he could see a beautiful garden with lawns, hedges, flowers and fountains. He could also see palace guards in the distance.

He quickened his pace and moved the cart as far to the left of the opening as he could. He followed the bend in the path trying not to be seen by the palace guards.

After the opening to the garden, the buildings that formed the alley gave way to high stone walls. The wall to his right bordered the garden and had flowering vines growing along the top. The wall to his left was much taller than the garden wall to his right. He could see spikes pointing up from the top of this wall.

That's the outside wall, thought Brock, looking up at the spikes.

I must be inside the palace grounds.

He stopped pushing the cart and listened. He could not hear shouts or running, or any other sound of pursuit.

Brock smiled and again began pushing the fish cart. He was not exactly relaxed now, but was a little more confident in his plan.

Far ahead, Brock could see that the alley turned a sharp right corner. He could see nothing more ahead after that. Carefully, Brock continued pushing the cart.

After a few more minutes Brock spied a second opening in the alley, just before the alley branched right.

If I understood the guards correctly, thought Brock, *that must lead to the kitchen.*

He slowed his pace, listening and watching for anything that might be danger.

Through the opening he saw a long low building with large open doors, dirty windows and a long portico. The building had several chimneys all of which billowed smoke. There were also a number of smaller out buildings. No one could be seen around any of them. Meats and fish hung on racks drying in the desert sun. A large vegetable garden was planted off in the distance.

Between where Brock stood and the long building was a large iron pot sitting on an unattended fire. Steam curled up from the contents of the black pot.

The sound of horses startled Brock. They came from around the bend in the alley.

Brock could do nothing more than quickly push the cart into the kitchen compound. He stopped it as close to the wall as he could and hid under the branches of a large tree.

Silently, Brock watched as two palace guards on horseback lazily walked along the alley. He dared not move or even breathe until they had passed from view. The guards looked neither left nor right.

Those two guards and the two at the gate need to find new jobs, thought Brock, smiling to himself.

"You there," came a voice from behind.

Brock jumped at the sound and slowly turned around.

"What are you doing there?"

The voice came from a very short, round man. The man was dressed in a greasy apron that, at one time, must have been white.

His creeks were red and he wore a permanent scowl on his face. As he spoke, he waved a large wooden spoon at Brock.

Brock smiled and pointed to the fish cart.

"Fish," he said, lamely.

"You don't expect to deliver fish under that tree, do ya?" shouted the man.

It was not really a question.

"Bring 'em on over there," said the man shaking his head in disgust.

He pointed the spoon at a small building that sat near the vegetable garden.

"I swear they get dumber every day," complained the man.

Grumbling to himself, the man lumbered back into the main kitchen building.

Brock smiled and slowly pushed the cart through the compound to where the man had pointed. He stopped next to a low bench and a table which looked like it was used for cleaning fish. A barrel of water stood near the table. Flies swarmed all around and the smell of rotten fish was unmistakable.

Brock left the cart and casually took a step or two along the side of the building. He looked over his shoulder to make sure he was not being watched. Keeping the little building between himself and a view of the kitchen, Brock began running toward the vegetable garden. He ran as quickly as he could. As soon as he entered the garden he ducked down behind a row of tall bush bean plants.

Brock listened carefully, but could hear nothing but his own heavy breathing. He peered up from behind the row of plants. There was no one to be seen. Brock ran, bent over, along the row of bush bean plants. Once he was deep within the vegetable garden, he slowed his pace and stood normally.

Carefully, he found his way to the wall that bordered the kitchen compound. He found an opening in the wall, a breach really, and squeezed through it.

This part of the alleyway was dirt. It wasn't really an alley any more, but a little road that allowed guards to patrol the perimeter of the palace. It was bordered by the outer and inner palace walls.

Brock peered up and down the road. He could see many sets of hoof prints in the dirt but no guards or horses in either direction.

I wonder how often the guards come along this road, he asked himself, silently?

If I go along the road and they come, I'll have nowhere to hide. He looked forward and then back the other direction and shook his head.

He quickly squeezed back through the opening in the wall and looked around to get his bearings. He could see past the vegetable garden to the wall that separated it from the Woman's Garden. He could also see the tall buildings that make up the palace itself and the living quarters of the Favored Ones.

"Breaking into the palace today should be easier than it was last night," he said smiling to himself. "Getting them out, now that's going to be something else altogether."

જી   જી   જી   જી   જી

The ride to the King's palace was never a pleasant one for Prince Rhala'nn. He hated the long road that led from the city. He hated the desert on either side of the road that led up to the palace. It was an engineering marvel for Porco to have built a stone road through desert sand.

Most of all, the prince hated the majestic view his father enjoyed from this mountaintop fortress. It was the highest point in the entire kingdom.

The King prided himself in being able to see the desert and the sea and everything else in Saalespor from this kingly home. Rhala'nn hated it because it wasn't his view, his home or his kingdom.

"Why have you brought me here like a virtual prisoner?" demanded the Prince.

What he did not yet understand was that there was nothing virtual about it.

General Ryguy Roces did not answer.

He was tall, strong and loyal; everything the prince was not. He was as handsome as he was trustworthy.

The general had counseled the King against the wickedness of the prince with his Spotters and Takers and unfortunate Favored Ones. He had warned the King about the growing threat of the prince's personal guard and his clear ambitions for the throne.

The King finally listened to his steadfast general about the time *The Black Claw* returned to the harbor. If it had not been for General Ryguy Roces, the King would have eventually perished in some tragic accident or mysterious illness and Saalespor would have plunged even deeper into despair.

Rhala'nn groaned as General Ryguy Roces rode at the head of his guards. The morning sun glistened off his close-cropped red hair and spotless uniform. He rode with a dignity and purpose well beyond his years.

The general approached the steep lane that led to the main fortress gates and stopped. The entire way up to the gates was lined with horsemen in full battle gear, holding lances festooned with the King's colors. He had ordered this show of force and fidelity just before leaving to fetch the prince. General Ryguy Roces smiled slightly.

This will be a good day, he thought; *a day to remember.*

As if by command the general's guards moved their horses close to the prince. He realized, too late, that he was now tightly boxed in and could not escape no matter what he tried.

The insult and inconvenience of this excursion enraged the prince.

For this, someone will pay with pain, he promised himself.

It still had not occurred to Rhala'nn that he himself was in danger of paying with pain. It did occur to him, however, once he had passed through the massive front gates and entered the Common Courtyard.

In the center of the courtyard, surrounded by countless soldiers, was a man hanging from a tall scaffold. His wrists were tied to the crossbeam. He was shirtless and covered in sweat. Tied to his ankles, legs, knees and waist were large open leather bags. He hung there in agony; the weight of the bags pulling mercilessly on his shoulders and legs. The bottom of the lowest bag was less than a foot above the ground, but it didn't matter. As long as the bags didn't touch the ground, their full weight pulled cruelly on the man.

Soldiers walked past the man carrying baskets of sand. Each one shouted his own name, swore allegiance to the King and poured the sand from his basket into one of the bags hanging from the man. The added weight caused the man to cry out in anguish, for his joints were already stretched beyond endurance.

Rhala'nn looked away, bored. He had seen it a thousand times before. Then, something about the man's face suddenly struck the prince. He looked back at the man and realized the face frozen in agony belonged to the captain of his personal guard.

The man slowly turned his head and locked eyes with the prince. Calling upon what little strength he had left, the man took a deep breath and spat at the prince.

The crowd roared its approval.

Everything else after that was a blur for the prince until he found himself in the Upper Courtyard, standing before his father.

ᎢᏃ ᎢᏃ ᎢᏃ ᎢᏃ ᎢᏃ

"I don't know what she was thinking," replied Cilantra for the second time. "But, whatever it was, Lee'a has really helped us."

Cilantra stood on the terrace with an empty sack at her feet. Next to it laid a large coil of red silk rope.

She looked at the rope and then at the pile of red silk cord she had been braiding.

"This is exactly what I was trying to make," said Cilantra; "only longer and stronger."

"Can you slow down a little?" asked Brittany. "I never understood what you were making, or why."

"I have a plan," said Cilantra.

"I know," replied Brittany, trying to sound positive, but failing.

"You said you had a plan, but you never told me what it was." Brittany sat on the chase lounge, trying not to cry from frustration.

"Then the girls came and then they left, and then Lee'a sent this rope." Brittany took a deep breath.

"What could she have been thinking?" asked Brittany.

"I don't know what she was thinking," replied Cilantra for a third time. "But, I know what I am thinking."

"I don't," said Brittany, strongly.

Cilantra sat next to her uneasy friend and smiled sweetly.

"We're going to use the rope to climb down from the terrace and out of the palace. We're going to escape," whispered Cilantra.

Her face was a canvas of excited confidence.

"And then what?" asked Brittany.

"And then we'll find Falcon, or whoever left the cap, the flower and the three-step thorns," answered Cilantra sincerely. "They're sure to have a boat."

As she stood, Cilantra picked up the coil of rope.

"Help me tie the rope around this post," she said to Brittany.

"You think we are going to escape right now?" exclaimed Brittany.

"No," laughed Cilantra. "I think we're going to have breakfast right now," she said.

"But first, I want to see if this rope goes all the way to the ground or if we need to add some of the rope I made."

Still a little shocked, Brittany decided it would be easier to talk to Cilantra over breakfast. Since she was determined to measure the rope before having breakfast, the best thing to do, in

Brittany's mind, was to help tie the rope around the post.

"Alright," agreed Brittany. "But I am not climbing down that rope until we have made some better plans."

Cilantra looked at her friend sideways.

"Of course not," she laughed. "Do you think I'm crazy?"

Brittany decided it best not to answer that question. She stood and helped Cilantra tie the rope tightly around a post that held up the terrace roof.

They walked to the waist-high wall that bordered the terrace and looked down. Below was the small dirt road used by guards on patrol. Cilantra and Brittany looked carefully to the right and to the left. No one was on the road for as far as they could see.

Cilantra held the coil of rope in both hands. She looked around one last time and then threw the rope over the terrace wall.

Brittany and Cilantra watched the coil of rope tumble through the air and land on the ground.

"Great," cried Cilantra. "It's long enough!"

Without further comment, Cilantra turned away from the terrace wall and walked into the sitting room.

Brittany looked at the rope and then at her friend.

"Where are you going?" she asked in a voice filled with surprise.

"Let's have breakfast before the tea gets cold," answered Cilantra.

It seemed to her to be the most reasonable thing to do.

"Aren't you afraid someone will see the rope?" asked Brittany.

She began to wonder if maybe she was still asleep and this was all just a bad dream.

"The guards never come by," replied Cilantra with a laugh. "And even if they did," she continued, "they are so lazy they wouldn't even notice."

Picking up the teapot, Cilantra asked, "Honey?"

"What did you say?" asked Brittany.

"Do you want honey in your tea?"

"Oh, yes, thank you," answered Brittany blankly.

This has got to be a bad dream, she thought to herself.

ଓ   ଓ   ଓ   ଓ   ଓ

Carefully, quietly, Brock moved through the far edge of the Woman's Garden, as he had the night before. It was easier to hide in the dark of night than it was now in daylight.

He slowly made his way through bush and hedge to a low wall that marked where the garden ended. It was built next to a large tree and seemed forgotten.

Brock listened for any sound that might warn him someone was near. All was perfectly still. Using a low hanging tree branch, Brock pulled himself up into the tree and then onto the top of the wall. He carefully moved along the top of the wall until it connected with the palace itself.

Brock stopped, listened and looked all around. Nothing moved but the smoke curling from the kitchen chimneys in the distance.

"I just need to do this one more time," Brock said to himself.

With all his strength, he jumped up. He made it high enough to grab roof tiles on the palace portico; they held. Without making a sound, he pulled himself up and onto the roof.

With cat-like swiftness, he ran up and over the roof until he came to the ocean side of the palace. From there he could see balcony after balcony, terrace upon terrace all facing the sea. Below was the dirt road that formed the perimeter of the palace grounds.

Last night, with the cover of darkness, he had been able to jump unseen from terrace to terrace until he found Cilantra's suite. Now, however, in the morning light, he was sure he would be spotted if he tried that again.

I can't stay up here all day until it gets dark, thought Brock, *so I have to risk the road.*

He carefully made his way to the edge of the roof and began looking as far as he could up and down the dirt road below. He could see that it curved sharply before proceeding along the wall under all the terraces. He carefully moved closer to the rim then stuck his head over the edge of the roof.

Brock froze. His heart jumped into his throat. Directly below him were two guards slowly riding their horses around the curve and under the terraces.

They neither talked nor moved their heads, but rode as if half asleep.

Brock silently moved his head out of view and listened; nothing. He was safe, or so he thought.

The good thing about this, thought Brock, *is the guards won't be back this way for a long time. I'll have time to get into Cilantra's room.*

Brock looked up and down the road, again. Satisfied that he could not be seen by the guards, he quietly lowered himself onto the dirt road.

ℭ   ℭ   ℭ   ℭ   ℭ

Cilantra picked up the last piece of orange on the tray.

"Do you mind?" she asked politely.

"Go right ahead," replied Brittany. "There's another orange on the breakfast tray we brought from my room," she added.

Cilantra popped the orange wedge into her mouth, savoring the sweet juice as it trickled down her throat.

"I still don't understand how you think we'll find Falcon, or whoever left the cap," said Brittany.

She picked up a small piece of flat bread and put it into her mouth. As she chewed, she tried to think of the right words to tell Cilantra that the plan was not really well thought out.

"I've been thinking," said Brittany.

"Shhhh," said Cilantra, putting her finger up to her lip.

"No," replied Brittany, gently. "I think we need to plan things a little better before we go climbing down that rope."

"Shhhhh," said Cilantra again; "Listen!"

She was looking in the direction of the terrace with an expression of fear frozen on her face.

When Brittany looked at the terrace she could see that the rope was stretched tight and moved a little. Scraping sounds and muffled groans could be heard coming from below.

"Someone is climbing up the rope from the road below!" whispered Brittany in alarm. "I told you not to leave it there."

"Maybe it is Falcon," replied Cilantra, hopefully.

She stood and took a step toward the terrace. Just then, a huge hand with fat sausage-like fingers reached up and over the terrace wall.

"It's not Falcon," cried Brittany. "It's a Porco!"

A second fat hand grabbed the top of the terrace wall. With much straining and noise, the head of a guard came into view.

Brittany screamed, but Cilantra just kept walking into the terrace.

"What are you doing with this here rope?" demanded the guard. He struggled to get himself over the wall.

As Cilantra walked toward the guard, she took a small leather pouch from her pocket.

It had just been an hour before that she had cut thorns from the twig and carefully put them into the leather pouch. She had no way of knowing they would be needed so soon.

Opening the pouch, she cautiously removed one long three-step thorn and held it between her thumb and forefinger.

"A jewel encrusted cage is still a cage!" said Cilantra. "We will not be imprisoned, even in silk," she declared.

Cilantra took a deep breath and jabbed the guard's hand with the thorn.

"Hey!" cried the guard. "Watch what yur doing with that."

A strange expression came over the guard's face and his eyes rolled back in his head. His hands trembled and then lost their grip on the top of the terrace wall. Without another sound, the man fell backward from the terrace.

ଔ   ଔ   ଔ   ଔ   ଔ

The Greens from *Advocate* were the first wave to land on the precious sands of Saalespor. Lord Reed and the faithful Lieutenant Hogan sloshed through the surf with the primary landing party.

"No disrespect intended, Lord Reed," said Lieutenant Hogan, "but our green uniforms do us no good here, sir."

"Please explain," replied Reed as he signaled for troops to deploy along a tall sandy berm.

"Our men," began Hogan; "*Your* men," he corrected himself, "are accustomed to hiding in places filled with trees and dense foliage."

Half-way through his words Hogan realized that Lord Reed knew much more about how and where the Greens hid than he did. Taking a deep breath, he continued anyway.

"Here," said Hogan, gesturing around the beach, "with the white ocean sand and the red desert sand beyond, our green uniforms can be spotted from miles away."

"Thank you, Lieutenant," replied Reed, not unkindly. "We did not have time or supplies to make new uniforms," continued Reed, "but we do have canvas sailcloth."

As he spoke, Reed pointed to the tall sandy berm which had been swarming with men in green just moments before. Now, it looked deserted.

"I don't understand," said Hogan, wishing he had not said anything at all.

"Watch," replied Reed. He pointed to a ridge toward which dozens of men were running. The Greens could easily be seen as they ran, but when they got to the sandy ridge, some of them pulled sailcloth from their backpacks. These men spread the sailcloth over the sand. All the men began quickly throwing sand on top of the canvases, covering it with a thin layer. In moments, they all burrowed underneath the canvas and disappeared.

Reed smiled.

"You were right, Lieutenant," he said. "Green is not a good color for hiding in sand. I see now why Captain Balworth speaks so highly of you."

Hogan blushed.

"Yes, sir," he replied. "Thank you, sir."

"Please find Captain Balworth," ordered Reed, "and inform him the Reds are landing ahead of schedule."

"Yes sir," Hogan replied smartly.

"Tell him also that some of the Yellows have already landed."

"Right away, sir," replied Hogan as he ran off to find Captain Balworth.

Reed gave his full attention to the beach. He could see Shank's archers in their bright yellow uniforms taking positions along with his own troops. Falcon's Reds were starting to join them.

Green, yellow or red, it makes no difference. Until they are hidden in the sand, thought Reed, *they are all too easy to spot.*

All up and down the shore, as far as he could see, troops were jumping from landing boats and running up the beach, only to disappear under a blanket of sand.

Sometimes the simplest solution is the best solution, he reminded himself.

As he made his way through the surf his feet became tangled in some torn rigging. He looked around to find the water full of flotsam that had once been a ship.

"This can't be one of ours," Reed said aloud.

Gazing out to sea, he could see that most of the fleet was deployed along the shore invading the precious sands of Saalespor.

"At least I hope it's not one of ours," he added, a frown darkening his face.

Turning back toward shore, Reed made his way through the debris to land. Looking around, the frown on his face was replaced by a grateful smile.

The invading troops were perfectly synchronized with all the parts doing exactly what they were supposed to do.

This is going better than any of us expected, thought Reed. He was sure the Lord Hiram would be pleased.

Reed ran as quickly as he could to the foot of a nearby plateau. He continued up a steep path hoping to get as good a view of the beach as possible. He stopped running near the top and turned to survey the invasion.

Longboats lined the shore. They came filled with troops and then went back empty to get more. Though unseen, Reed knew the perimeter of the beachhead was now guarded by hundreds of troops hidden in the sand. Hundreds more were landing, forming up in ranks, ready to march on the harbor.

Surprise is our friend, thought Reed with a smile. *They won't know we're here until it's too late.*

Reed watched specially designed flat boats ferry horses from *Trident*. The cavalry had worked hard to rebuild after Kyler and his lancers were slaughtered at Three Rivers.

"Oh, brother," said Reed softly. "You would be so proud of them."

As Reed watched the first group of horses jump from the flat boats and swim through the shallow surf, something caught his attention.

On the breeze was the slightest scent of sweaty horsehair.

That's not possible, thought Reed.

He was about to laugh at himself, when he again caught the scent of horsehair.

He turned and glanced up the slope on which he stood. Above him, the path led to a plateau.

Now, without a doubt, Reed again smelled horse sweat; then came the unmistakable sound of a hoof stamp and a snort.

That's not possible, thought Reed, again. *Our cavalry is just landing now.*

Ever so quietly, Lord Reed, ninth son of the House of Hiram, pulled out his sword.

CHAPTER 6
A Very Special Day

*B*rock stood perfectly still and listened.

How long do I have to wait here, he wondered?

He wanted desperately to peek around the curve to see how far the guards had traveled. He was also not sure what to do if he was spotted by the guards.

The inner palace wall was almost impossible for him to climb over, but he could do it. He would have to escape that way if need be. The outer palace wall was simply too high to climb, plus it had spikes and sharp things imbedded in the top.

What about the girls, wondered Brock? *Getting them out; now that's going to be harder than I thought.*

It just occurred to him that if he had a hard time climbing the inner wall, Cilantra and Brittany may not be able to climb it at all.

"I thought we would all go out the same way I came in;" he continued talking to himself; "the same way I went out last night."

He now realized he might be totally unable to get them out of the palace.

Not too bright of you to start thinking about this now, he chided himself.

Frustrated, he decided to take a chance and peek up the road to see how far the guards had gotten. He listened carefully before moving forward. We could hear water from a fountain and birds singing their morning song, but no sound came from road ahead.

Brock moved around the curve in the road as slowly and silently as possible. He pressed himself flat against the inner wall, both arms down; palms flush against the wall and slowly slid one side-step at a time. When he passed the curve, he cocked his head slightly and looked.

At first, Brock could not understand what he was seeing. In a moment or two he realized there were two horses standing near the inner wall without riders. Brock took a step forward and then another. As he gazed at the horses he saw that the riders were on the ground at the horses' feet, lying as if dead.

Carefully, slowly, Brock crept toward the men and horses. Nothing moved at first until one horse pulled back his ears.

"Oh, there boy," said Brock in a soft low voice.

The horse moved his ears forward and took a careful step over one of the bodies. The other horse stood still with his head lowered and nudged the body of the other guard.

"Oh, there boy," said Brock again, soft and low. "Don't wake him up."

The horse eyed Brock for a moment and then took a step or two closer to the other horse. Brock looked carefully at the guards; neither was breathing.

It was then he noticed a red rope hanging from the terrace above.

ભ   ભ   ભ   ભ   ભ

Reed carefully moved up the path, trying to see who or what was on the plateau without being seen. He could not see much, but he saw enough to confirm that two horses were standing at the edge the plateau. He was sure they were not from the House of Hiram.

Slowly, Reed turned around on the steep path and sat facing the sea. Thankfully, it was a bright and sunny morning. He took his sword and tried to signal the men on the beach by flashing sunlight on its shiny blade. No one seemed to notice.

Reed tried to shift his position to be more easily seen from below, but as he did, the ground on the path gave way. He slipped down several feet. Rocks and dirt noisily careened down the path. Thankfully, he was able to stop himself by digging in his heals. Daring not to move, he listened for any sound from above.

It was then he noticed flashes of light coming from the beach. One of Herald's men was using a signal mirror.

At first, Reed tried to signal back that they all were being watched from the plateau by two men on horseback. It was too complicated a message. Finally, he just signaled his name and the code for help.

Herald's man began running toward Reed, apparently shouting, though he was too far away for Reed to hear. Moments later, however, others did hear. The sandy berm nearest Reed's path erupted as a cadre of men jumped out from hiding under sailcloth.

Reed distinctly heard the horses above him being turned and kicked to start running.

"Yaaaa! Yaaaa!" shouted the Porco riders.

Reed stood waving his sword and shouted, "Archers to me! Archers to me!"

Up the path came five of Reed's men in green and three of Shank's archers in bright yellow.

Pointing up the path Reed shouted, "Stop those horsemen!"

The archers flew past Reed, arrows on strings. When they arrived at the top of the path the three archers stood and let fly a volley of arrows, and another, and yet again a third.

The fate of the secret invasion was now a race between nine arrows and two horsemen.

Without waiting a moment longer, Reed ran down the path until he found Herald's signalman.

"Signal the fleet we have been discovered," cried Reed. "Tell *Fyrmatus* and *Tempest* to take the harbor, immediately!"

Then, as if to himself he added, "Falcon and Ram will know what to do."

ღ   ღ   ღ   ღ   ღ

"Are you ready to go?" asked Cilantra.

She was pacing back and forth in the sitting room and kept looking at the rope hanging from the terrace.

"I don't know," replied Brittany. "I just don't know." Her voice was on the border between panic and despair.

Both Brittany and Cilantra were still in shock at the appearance of the guard on the terrace, but Brittany was inclined to stop, think and regroup, while Cilantra wanted to take action; something, anything.

"How do you know there are not more Porco guards, or palace guards, or gardeners, or, or, or whatever?" asked Brittany.

"I know the sooner we go, the less chance there is we will get caught," replied Cilantra.

"How do you know that?" asked Brittany.

She, too, kept looking at the terrace.

"The guards don't come by very often," answered Cilantra. "But they do come by."

"Eventually," she continued, trying to keep her composure, "someone will come and find their, find their…"

Cilantra could not bring herself to say 'find their bodies'.

"…and find them," she said, finally.

"We can't go," said Brittany, her voice trembling.

"I know it's frightening," began Cilantra.

"We can't go," said Brittany, interrupting Cilantra in mid-sentence.

Cilantra looked at Brittany wanting to offer words of comfort, but seeing her friend made the hairs on the back of her neck tingle.

Brittany was pale white with eyes wide in fright. Trembling, she was pointing toward the terrace.

The red rope tied to the post was again pulled tight and again was moving. Scraping noises could be heard coming up from the wall. Someone was again climbing the rope.

Without waiting a second, Cilantra opened her small leather pouch and carefully extracted a poisonous thorn.

She then calmly walked to the terrace wall, waiting for a hand to appear.

Brittany saw it all happening again, as if in a slow moving nightmare. A hand came up grasping the top of the terrace wall. Cilantra purposefully raised the thorn, holding it firmly between her thumb and forefinger.

As she was about to strike, the man's other hand grasped the top of the wall.

It was then Brittany knew; she knew for certain.

"Stop!" cried Brittany. "No Porco."

"Stop!" she cried again. "No Porco."

They were all the words her mouth would say.

Cilantra's hand acted as if it had a mind of its own. It moved down to prick the man's hand even as her mind heard Brittany's warning.

"Stop!" Brittany cried again; "stop!"

Cilantra, unable to stop the motion of her hand, at the last minute tossed the thorn aside, poking the man only with her finger.

A friendly and definitely non-Porco face came up over the terrace wall.

"Hello," said the face. "My name's Brock. May I come in?"

Not waiting for an answer, Brock scrambled over the terrace wall.

Cilantra and Brittany backed away from the strange man they had let climb onto their terrace.

He stopped moving and put both hands up, palms out, trying to appear harmless.

"I'm here to rescue you," he said, smiling widely. "Falcon sent me."

"Falcon?" cried Cilantra.

Brock looked at Cilantra and nodded happily. Then, looking toward Brittany he added, "and Quasar, too."

ଔ   ଔ   ଔ   ଔ   ଔ

The two horsemen rode madly to sound the alarm that the precious sands of Saalespor were in danger. They had no idea that their own precious lives were also in danger. Shank's archers watched from the plateau as their nine arrows rained down on the unsuspecting riders.

The first rider was struck by the first arrow and fell from his horse. The second rider pulled brutally on his horse's reigns. He frantically swerved to miss crashing into the riderless horse. In so doing, he also managed to avoid the other arrows. They struck where he had been riding just moments before.

The fortunate rider violently kicked his horse and rode straight for the signal tower in the harbor. There was nothing left to stop him from igniting the signal flame.

Herald's trumpeters blared on the beach, their message being repeated by shouts from officers and troops up and down the beachhead. In response, all of the men that were hidden emerged from their sandy hollows.

From the plateau the beach looked like a rainbow of colored feathers in a windstorm. Men seemed to swirl in meaningless groups of red, green, yellow and silver, but those who watched knew better.

The Greens and Yellows on the plateau ran down the path to join their units, for the armies of the House of Hiram were on the move.

Flagmen on the beach signaled the fleet. Immediately, all remaining long boats were lowered. The ships then unfurled their sails and weighed anchor. None waited for the empty boats to return from shore.

One by one the ships followed *Fyrmatus* and *Tempest* to the unsuspecting harbor.

Reed gave the order for units to gather on the plateau as soon as they were able. Immediately, colorful-coded groups swarmed up the hill and assembled on the plateau.

From this vantage point the entire road to the harbor could be seen. Coarse reddish-brown desert sand and fine white beach sand bordered the road.

The cavalry was the last to assemble on the plateau. They stood at the back of the formation. The lancers would guard the rear from attack while still being able to charge forward if needed.

All the Lord Hiram's men stood at the ready. The left and right flanks were manned with the Greens. The Reds stood, as usual, at the front; behind them were Shank's archers. Scattered throughout were the Sky Blue uniforms of Herald's signalmen.

Lords Reed, Shank and Herald stood together at the front of the formation. They looked around one more time to be sure all was in order. Reed caught sight of the armada sailing rapidly toward the harbor. *Vengeance* and *Scorpion* followed in the distance.

This will be a good day, he thought; *a day to remember*.

Reed signaled his readiness with a slight nod of the head. Shank did likewise. Herald smiled and motioned to his trumpeters. They sounded such a furious flurry that it echoed out to sea and into the desert. Sailors on the ships cheered when they heard it. Mothers in town called their children home. A lone fisherman sitting near the seawall stopped mending his nets and looked worriedly toward the sky. The men on the plateau joined in with a furious shout of their own and then moved forward as one.

Something caught the fisherman's eye. Two warships rapidly approached the mouth of the harbor. The man squinted to see details of the ships.

"They're not from Saalespor," said the man. No one was near to hear.

He watched as the ships lowered their mainsails and glided into the harbor. They both flew flags bearing Twin Black Hawks; one on a field of red and the other purple.

The fisherman dropped his nets and stood to watch the warships. The purple-flagged ship took a position in the mouth of the harbor. The red-flagged ship made her way toward the deep water docks.

Suddenly, the sound of a horse rapidly approaching caused the fisherman to turn his gaze from the sea. A lone rider rode madly onto the seawall. He didn't slow his pace even when he got to the slippery wet stone pathway. The man was finally forced to slow down when his horse skidded and he almost lost his seat.

Jumping from the horse the soldier ran the rest of the way to the tower.

Aboard *Fyrmatus*, Lord Falcon turned his attention from the docks to the seawall.

"Archers to me," he shouted.

Mr. Schooper rang the bell briskly and shouted,

"Archers on deck!"

"Archers on deck!"

A cadre of men in yellow ran to the quarter deck.

Pointing toward the figure running along the seawall Falcon shouted, "Stop that man!"

Instantly, in one smooth action, the archers strung their bows. They then ran to the starboard side of the ship, putting arrow to string.

On the seawall a soldier ran with all his might toward the tower. He arrived at the tower door as a silent volley of arrows flew from *Fyrmatus.*

Captain Hacim Roces, younger brother of General Ryguy Roces pulled on the tower door. It refused to open. Placing one foot on the base of the tower and grabbing the door ring with both hands, Captain Roces pulled with all his strength. The door opened just as arrows met their mark.

Several arrows struck the open door which acted as an accidental shield. Others clattered harmlessly on the stone pavement. Captain Roces cried out in pain as at least one arrow found him. He stumbled, wounded, into the tower.

Aboard *Tempest*, Lord Ram had already given orders to strike the tower. Ram was skilled in building machines of war. One of his great catapults was already positioned on deck. Men pulled mightily on the gears that winched the arm and bucket.

Ram smiled as his men loaded it with boulders that had been shipped for just a moment as this.

"Turn her port 10 degrees," Ram shouted. Men pull and pushed the rollers to adjust exactly where the catapult faced. Aiming such a weapon required a skill that few but Ram possessed.

Satisfied, Ram shouted, "Clear the base." He wanted to be sure no one stood where they could be mangled by the arm and bucket.

Ram took a deep breath, and nodded to himself.

"Release," his deep voice bellowed.

With a great mechanical noise and shouts from the crew, the machine launched its payload into the air. A strange silence blanketed the ship as all eyes watched the stones fly toward the tower.

Two great stones soared through the air each following their own trajectory. One seemed to be right on target, but it crashed harmlessly into the seawall at the base of the tower. The smaller stone overshot the tower and splashed blandly into the harbor.

Ram knew that the shape, size and weight of stones cause them to fly differently. When used against a fortress wall, any stone will usually hit something, but hitting a solitary tower requires a good aim and good fortune.

Falcon watched Ram's efforts from the deck of *Fyrmatus.*

Maybe the arrows did their job, he thought, hopefully.

A moment or two later he knew they had failed when a wisp of black smoke curled from the top of the tower.

ଔ   ଔ   ଔ   ଔ   ଔ

"How dare you!" shouted, General Ryguy Roces. "The King asked you a question. Do you not answer him?"

Rhala'nn blinked wildly at the harsh sound of the general's voice. It was as if he were awakening from a deep sleep. He was surprised to find himself standing in the Upper Courtyard. Before him were the royal dais and his father's throne. Rhala'nn blinked again and tried to focus.

"Where is my throne," he mumbled?

The dais was minus the customary second throne; the one that had belonged to his mother. Rhala'nn had claimed it for his own the day his mother died. The King had been too grief stricken to reprimand his son's impertinent ambition, and the courtiers too weak.

"Father," said Rhala'nn, his disrespect returning. "Where is my throne?"

"Your mother's throne," answered the King, bitterly. Rising from his throne, the King continued poignantly; "It is no longer needed."

"Hear me," shouted the King. "It is I who am asking the questions today!"

King Ahala'nn stepped toward his son.

"You will answer me."

Rhala'nn blinked again and tried to calm himself. His father had never spoken to him like this; never.

"Fezala," shouted Rhala'nn, summoning his personal aide; "a drink – bring me wine."

Instinctively, General Ryguy Roces raised his hand to strike this impertinent son, but he was the son of a king, nonetheless. The general held his hand in check and glanced at King Ahala'nn.

A look of deep sadness crossed the King's face. He nodded his consent to General Ryguy Roces and turned away to sit again upon his throne.

The blow was not even half of what it could have been, yet it served its purpose. The prince found himself face down in the courtyard dirt; no longer impudent.

The taste of his own blood and the spots of light swirling before his eyes were incomprehensible to him.

"Now stand and answer the King," growled General Ryguy Roces.

The prince had never been struck in all of his life. He had rarely known discomfort of any kind. The pursuit of pleasure and the avoidance of discomfort was the sum of his life. Pain was a rude awaking.

He pulled himself to his feet and started to shout at the King.

"Who is this animal who would dare to strike…"

The King again rose to his feet. The general again raised his hand, this time clenched in a fist.

"Are you so slow to learn," asked the King, "that you need another lesson?"

The expression of solid resolve on the King's face was unknown to Rhala'nn.

He glanced at the general's raised fist and tasted anew the blood from his split lip.

Rhala'nn shook his head, 'No'.

"You will speak when the King asks you a question," snarled the general. There was a deep anger in his voice.

"I don't need another lesson," replied Rhala'nn, glaring furiously at his father.

"Whom do you address," hissed the general. The last of his restraint was vanishing.

"I don't need another lesson, *Father*," repeated Rhala'nn, sarcastically.

The King tiredly sat upon his throne and starred at his son.

"Today, I am your King, not your father," proclaimed Ahala'nn. "You will address me as such."

All eyes were upon Rhala'nn. He knew there was something expected of him, but he could not understand what it was. Finally, the words came to him.

"I don't need another lesson, *Your Majesty*," said Rhala'nn.

Though spoken with feigned humility, his rehabilitation had begun.

"Answer me then," commanded the King. "I'll ask you again. What is the purpose of your Spotters and Takers?"

Is that what this is all about, thought Rhala'nn?

"They bring me gifts from other lands, Your Majesty," began Rhala'nn with feigned deference.

From the right side of the Upper Courtyard came a line of men, hands tied behind their backs. There was a Spotter, a Taker (or Wagon Leader) and three Royal Guards.

Rhala'nn began to tremble at the sight.

The Spotter wore colorful silks from Rhala'nn's palace. He had very long black hair which was thickly oiled and pulled into a tightly braided ponytail. Pieces of bone, colorful shells, and shiny stones were woven into the braid.

The Taker was the complete opposite. He was strong in size and in smell, but not in mind. His face bore tattoos; patterns of dots and dashes crudely made with blue ink. His unkempt hair was matted with dirt as were the clothes he wore. The stench from this Porco fouled the air of the Upper Courtyard, causing Rhala'nn to gag.

The Royal Guards were very tall, strong men, even by Saalspor's standards; which is saying a lot. They wore red pants and thin black vests. Their bare arms and necks bulged with muscles. The sun glistened off their shaved, oiled heads.

All eyes watched the line of men as they were marched into the Upper Courtyard.

"Tell me more about these so called 'gifts' from other lands," commanded the King.

"Speak truth or pay with pain," whispered General Ryguy Roces.

Rhala'nn looked at the general, then at the line of men and then at the King.

"Your Majesty," began Rhala'nn, his voice smooth and confident. "I am sure you have more important matters to consider than what these servants bring from other lands."

At the word 'servants' the Spotter and Royal Guards turned their heads and glared at Rhala'nn. The Spotter's nostrils flared in anger. The Royal Guards' muscles twitched and throbbed.

"I am not interested in what you are sure about," shouted the King. "Tell me what these men bring you from other lands!" commanded the King.

Rhala'nn blinked uncontrollably. His father had never before spoken to him in this manner. He swallowed hard while thinking of what to say.

"I suggest," hissed General Ryguy Roces, "you tell the truth this time."

"Your Majesty," said Rhala'nn, weakly. "They bring Favored Ones to me; women who may become my wife and the mother of your grandchildren."

Rhala'nn smiled his brightest smile; sure he had touched his father's heart.

"These Favored Ones," asked the King. "They agree to come, their fathers agree, their mothers agree?"

"Your Majesty," answered Rhala'nn, in feigned innocence. "It is hard to know what these servants do while in foreign lands."

Were they not bound, the Spotter and the Royal Guards would have killed Rhala'nn where he stood. The Taker was confused by it all.

"A king must know what his subjects do at all times," said the King; "Servant or son, it matters not," continued the King, sadly. "I have learned this of late."

Rhala'nn starred at his father, but said nothing.

"Prince Rhala'nn," said the King, firmly; "You wish to be king?"

Rhala'nn's mind swirled at the various things he could say. His cheek began twitching uncontrollably.

"No, my lord," replied Rhala'nn, finally. A greater lie has never been spoken.

"I wish for you to live and rule forever," said the Prince.

"Yes, I'm sure," answered the King, dryly.

"Walk with me," commanded the King as he stepped down from the dais. "I would show you the kingdom as never before."

With a slight reassuring gesture, the King stopped General Ryguy Roces and his personal guard from accompanying them. Father and son walked slowly to the seaward edge of the Upper Courtyard and surveyed all that could be seen; the desert, the city and the sea.

No one heard the conversation, but the Prince did not look happy. Both the King and Rhala'nn looked intently in the distance. A long colorful line, red, green, yellow and silver, snaked its way along the ocean road toward the harbor.

"What is that in the harbor?" asked Rhala'nn. His voice was once again that of a spoiled child.

The King clutched his chest in disbelief. "Those are warships," answered the King. "Something you should recognize by this stage of your life," he said with disgust.

"What, all seven, eight, no nine of them?" asked the Prince, counting as he spoke.

The King and Prince eyed the unimaginable; warships in their harbor. King Ahala'nn then noticed black smoke billowing from the signal tower.

He turned and faced the courtyard so rapidly that his personal guard jumped in surprise.

"To arms," the King shouted. "We are under attack; to arms!"

His personal guard swarmed the King. Their only concern was for his safety. They were on him in a moment, forming a tight circle; shields as a wall, swords at the ready.

The circle moved the King slowly toward the safety of the inner fortress. These men would all die before allowing harm to come to the King. In the confusion, Prince Rhala'nn fell to the ground and was left behind.

Suddenly, the Upper Courtyard exploded with the sound of a running horse and shouts from palace guards.

Had the rider been unknown, he might have been killed, but General Ryguy Roces recognized him.

"Let him through," cried the general.

The rider stopped his horse directly in front of the general. Two arrows hung from the side of his saddle; another from his leg and two more from his arm and chest armor. He was wet in his own blood.

"General," said the man, weakly. "We are under attack from land and from sea."

Having so spoken, Captain Hacim Roces slipped from his horse and landed at the feet of his older brother.

The general motioned to his men. Instantly, trumpeters sounded the call to arms. The sound of their blast echoed throughout the palace fortress.

Horsemen and soldiers in the fortress flew into action. Those in the Common Courtyard stopped the pay-with-pain spectacle and ran to their posts. Archers manned the fortress walls and the heavy main gates were shut.

General Ryguy Roces knelt at the side of his bloodied brother.

"You have done well, Hacim," said General Ryguy Roces.

"Tell mother and father my last thoughts were of them," said Hacim, weakly. He closed his eyes as a raspy sound escaped from his mouth.

"Tell them yourself," pleaded Ryguy. "You will not die," commanded the general. "That is an order. You will not die."

Captain Hacim Roces' eyes fluttered open for a moment, "Yes sir," he answered, with a slight smile. His eyes then fluttered shut.

"Take him to the healers," cried General Ryguy Roces.

"But General," began one of the guards, "your brother, is..."

"I don't care," said the general sharply. "Take him to the healers!"

"Yes sir," answered the man, smartly.

Five men carefully lifted the limp body of Captain Hacim Roces and moved him from the Upper Courtyard.

"The Prince!" came a sudden cry.

General Ryguy Roces looked first to the King. He was still protected by the ring of shields.

The King had stopped his guards at the sound of the words. The general then looked around the courtyard to where the Prince lay motionless in the dirt.

Palace guards ran to the Prince. The first to arrive knelt quickly and examined him.

"There is blood," cried the guard. "He's been stabbed."

The King came running ahead of his guards. Kneeling at his son's side, he cried, "Rhala'nn, Rhala'nn, can you hear me?"

The guards formed a ring of shields around the King and his son. Facing outward, they could neither see nor hear the final moments.

Prince Rhala'nn slowly opened his eyes and starred angrily at his father.

"I would have been a much better king," he said defiantly.

"Perhaps," answered the King. "But I still have time to right many wrongs."

"Unlike me," laughed the Prince. He coughed up a throat full of blood.

"When you see her," said the King, gently, "tell your mother I love her still."

"She will not see me," said the Prince.

"Yes, yes," replied the King. "She will comfort you. You will be fine," said the King, softly. "She will greet you on the other side."

"She will not," spat the insolent Prince. "It was I who poisoned her," declared Rhala'nn with an evil smile. "And you were next."

Taking a deep breath, the King whispered his most closely held secret.

"My son," said the King, his face contorted in pain. "I know what you did to your mother and I know what you tried to do to me."

The King sobbed as he spoke. "I have always known and so did your mother."

The King bent low and spoke into Rhala'nn's ear. "Your mother forgave you even as she died in my arms. She begged me to forgive you, too. This is why you have lived until today."

The Prince coughed up more blood. Choking, he said, "I would have been a much better king;" And he breathed his last.

The King staggered to his feet.

"General," he cried. "My son has been killed."

General Ryguy Roces broke through the guards and ran to the King's side.

"How can this be?" asked the general. "No one came near him or the guards would have stopped them," he said, thinking aloud.

"Then the assassin must be one of the guards," cried the King, heatedly. "Search them all," ordered the King. "The one with the bloody dagger is the killer of my son."

The King staggered through the circle of guards to the edge of the Upper Courtyard. He dismissed them with a wave of his hand and looked out at the warships, the army and the burning tower.

"How could this have happened," he moaned.

Leaning against the fortress wall the King wept.

General Ryguy Roces could not believe one of his guards had killed the Prince, though he would have been happy to do the job, himself. Yet, the facts were undeniable.

He stood within the circle of guards.

"About face," ordered the general

In perfect unison the guards turned and faced the general in the center of the circle. He looked at each of his men. None had any blood on their uniforms.

"Hands out," he ordered.

The guards placed their shields on the ground and stood with both hands out facing the general. As he walked by, each man showed the general both sides of his hands. They all were bloodless.

"Weapons out," ordered the general.

Each man held his sword in one hand and his dagger in the other. As General Ryguy Roces faced them, they each flipped their weapons to reveal all sides of their bloodless blades.

The despondent king stopped crying and looked cautiously at the occupied general and the circle of guards.

Turning his back on them, he carefully retrieved a bloody dagger from its hiding place beneath his royal tunic. Glancing over his shoulder to make sure no one was watching, the King quickly threw the murder weapon over the fortress wall.

"Unlike you, my son" whispered the King. "I still have time to right many wrongs."

CB CB CB CB CB

"So, are you ready to go, yet?" asked Brock, patiently.

It was taking longer for them to leave than it did for him to convince Cilantra and Brittany that he was, indeed, there to rescue them.

"Just one more thing," implored Cilantra as she ran to the bedroom.

It was the third 'just-one-more-thing' of the morning.

She returned quickly from the bedroom holding something behind her back.

Brock looked at Cilantra's smiling face, then at Brittany and then back at Cilantra.

"What?" he asked, hesitantly.

"I think Falcon would want you to wear this," said Cilantra, quietly.

She handed him the red leather cap he had brought them from *Frymatus*.

"I know he will be grateful to you for rescuing us," continued Cilantra.

Looking at Brittany and then back at Brock, she added; "No matter what happens, we are grateful too."

"Thank you," replied Brock with true humility. "So, are you ready to go, yet" he asked again?

"One more thing," said Cilantra holding out her hand to Brittany.

"You don't want to leave this behind, do you?"

She handed Brittany a thin white ribbon. It was decorated by tiny embroidered flowers.

"Hey, I remember that!" cried Brock in surprise. "Quasar gave it to me so I could give it to you."

"The day we arrived," said Brittany, "someone in the crowd pressed it into my hand."

As Brittany spoke, a tear found its way down her cheek.

"I never saw who it was," she added.

"That was me," said Brock, happily.

"Yes," replied Brittany, smiling. "Yes, I know. Thank you."

"So, are we ready to go?" asked Brock yet again.

Yes," replied Cilantra.

"What are we waiting for?" asked Brittany.

Brock handed pieces of cloth he had ripped from the bed sheets to both of them.

"Wrap the cloths around your hands, like this," he explained, wrapping his own hands.

"They should protect your hands from getting burned by the rope, if you go down too fast."

Cilantra and Brittany both did as instructed.

"I'll carry the big backpack,' said Brock. "You each can carry one of the smaller ones."

"Are you sure we'll need them?" asked Brittany.

"No, I'm not," answered Brock, truthfully. "Maybe Falcon will find us soon, but if he does not, all that we will have to help us survive is what we carry."

Brock had packed the smaller backpacks with all the food he could find in their rooms. The girls had not seen what he had packed into the big backpack, but it was a lot heavier.

He didn't tell them his ship had been lost in the storm or that he didn't know how to find Falcon.

"Wait, just one more thing," said Cilantra.

Without waiting for a reply, she knelt, reached under a large settee and pulled out the piece of wood she had hidden there.

"Maybe you want this," she said, handing Brock the carved plank from *Emeraldsea*.

He slowly moved his fingers over the carved letters *'Emeral'*, the last remains of his precious ship.

"Where did you get this?" asked Brock, quietly.

"We found it in the surf just past the harbor," replied Brittany.

"I'm so sorry," added Cilantra.

Brock looked long and hard at the wooden plank. Setting it down on the settee, he closed his eyes for a moment and then took a deep breath.

"Look," he said with pointed directness; "I don't know how we are going to get back to Falcon and Quasar. But I do know the longer we wait here, the harder it will be."

Cilantra and Brittany both nodded silently. He looked at them square in the eyes and then continued.

"It's going to be hard. I won't blame you if you don't come with me, but I have to go."

Brock moved to the terrace.

"If they catch me here, I'm dead – you too, probably."

Brock put his hand on the red rope.

"So, are you ready to go?" he asked for the last time.

Cilantra and Brittany both smiled bravely.

"Yes," they said, at the same time.

"I'll go first, said Brock, "so I can be down on the ground to help when you both come down."

He didn't say, *so I can catch you if you fall*, which is what he was really thinking.

Without any more words, Brock looked over the terrace wall. The horses and guards were still there. He could see nothing else on the road in either direction.

"Don't wait," said Brock sternly. "Follow me right away."

With that, Brock straddled the wall, wrapped a leg around the rope, grabbed it with his hands, and slid easily to the road below.

Brock waved from below.

"Come on," he said, quietly. His smile was big and confident.

"After you," said Brittany, politely.

"Oh no," replied Cilantra, somewhat firmer than she had intended. "I insist; after you."

Brittany took a deep breath and then quickly did exactly what she had seen Brock do. It was easier than she had expected, and the cloth did help her hands.

"Good job," said Brock, excitedly.

He and Brittany both looked up, expecting to see Cilantra starting to come down on the rope.

She was not there.

Above in the room, a panicked expression darkened Cilantra's face. She stared at the door to the hallway, and then suddenly ran to it.

From the hallway came the distinct sound of tinkling bells. Cilantra quickly made sure the door was locked. The sound of tinkling bells grew louder, closer.

"Lee'a, is that you, honey?" asked Cilantra sweetly.

"Good morning," replied Lee'a cheerfully. The door handle rattled as she spoke.

"I've come for your breakfast trays. Are you finished?"

"Oh, I'm so sorry," replied Cilantra. "Brittany and I are busy with something," she continued truthfully. "Would you be a dear and come back at lunch time?"

"I won't disturb you, I promise," said Lee'a. "I'll just be a second."

"Lee'a you are such a friend." Cilantra spoke as if Lee'a had agreed. "You come at lunchtime, then. Thank you, dear."

"Fine," replied Lee'a.

She was used to following the whims of the Favored Ones.

Cilantra listened as the sound of tinkling bells disappeared down the hallway.

She turned and ran back to the terrace. Cilantra looked over the terrace wall only to be surprised by the face of Brock halfway up the rope.

"I'm sorry," said Cilantra, sincerely. "I'll explain when I get down there."

"You are coming down, then?" asked Brock.

"Yes, of course I am," replied Cilantra. She thought it was the oddest question.

"What else would I be doing?" she asked.

"I have no idea," chuckled Brock as he slid back down the rope.

Within moments the three were safe and sound on the dirt road.

"You see," began Cilantra. "Our breakfast trays were ready to be picked up by Lee'a."

"I really don't need to know," interrupted Brock. "We're all together now. That's what's important. We need to get going and we need to plan."

Brock grabbed the reigns of both horses, careful not to walk them over the guards' bodies.

"No but, really," began Cilantra, again.

"You didn't need to clean up our breakfast trays," interrupted Brittany, half in jest. "Really," she added, "sometimes you can be silly with all your cleaning."

Brittany smiled warmly at her friend, but her words stung a little.

"What?" asked Cilantra. "You don't understand," she said, trying to hold back her feelings. "That's not fair."

"I do understand that we need to get off of this road as soon as possible," replied Brock.

He tried to keep his voice light and friendly, but he felt they had already taken much too much time.

Hoping to move the conversation in another direction he asked,

"Which of you is the better rider?"

"I am," answered both girls.

Cilantra and Brittany looked at each other in surprise. Brittany laughed good-naturedly, but Cilantra did not.

"She is," said Brittany, correcting herself. She wanted to break the tension that had somehow come between them.

"Cilantra," said Brock. "If you will ride alone, Brittany can ride with me."

Cilantra nodded and tried to smile. She took the reins of one of the horses and started to mount the horse. Stopping with her foot in the stirrup she said; "Two things…"

Her tone was nice but there was firmness in it.

Brittany and Brock looked at Cilantra. A worried look came upon both of them.

"First," said Cilantra, quietly. "Brittany is just as good a rider as I am."

She looked at her friend with warm open eyes.

"If you want to ride alone," said Cilantra, "that's fine with me. You are a good rider."

Brittany smiled and began to say something in reply, but Cilantra just kept speaking.

"Second," she said seriously. "I was not cleaning breakfast trays or wasting time up there."

Brittany's smile faded at the sound of these words.

"Lee'a came to the door," explained Cilantra. Her voice cracked as she tried to keep herself from crying.

"I had to act quickly to stop her from coming in to get the trays," continued Cilantra, with difficulty. "If I hadn't, we would already be discovered."

Brittany moved rapidly to her friend and hugged her dearly. To keep herself from falling, Cilantra quickly pulled her foot from the stirrup. It spooked the horse, but Brock was able to grab its reigns.

"I'm sorry for saying what I said," replied Brittany. She too started crying.

"I'm sorry for worrying you and making you wait," replied Cilantra.

The two hugged and cried.

Brock looked at the horses, the bodies of the guards and up and down the road.

Men are much easier, he thought.

"You're right," said Cilantra, "I can be silly about cleaning up."

"Nonsense," replied Brittany, hugging her friend tightly.

The two girls stopped crying and started laughing.

"Ladies," said Brock with all the patience he could gather.

"We're standing on the road where the guards ride. We are trying to escape. If they find us, they will be very unhappy with us."

He paused to make sure his words were getting through. Cilantra and Brittany had stopped laughing. They were looking at him solemnly.

"I'm getting on this horse," declared Brock with what he hoped was a warm smile. As he spoke he slipped his foot into a stirrup and easily mounted the horse.

"One of you needs to get on behind me," he continued, "and the other needs to ride alone. Can we do that now?"

"Of course," said Cilantra.

"Why didn't you just say so," replied Brittany. She looked at Cilantra and grumbled, "Men!"

"He's just like Falcon," replied Cilantra.

They both broke out laughing.

"Do you want to ride alone, or with Brock," asked Cilantra?

"It doesn't matter," replied Brittany. "I just want to do whatever you want to do."

"It doesn't matter to me, either," replied Cilantra. "You are just as good a rider as I am, really you are."

"Ladies," said Brock, finally; "I hope you can keep up."

With that, he kicked his horse and began trotting up the road.

Cilantra and Brittany looked at Brock in jaw-dropping surprise.

"What's got into him," asked Brittany?

"Come on," said Cilantra as she mounted her horse. We can ride together."

Cilantra offered her hand to Brittany who jumped effortlessly onto the back of the horse.

Cilantra kicked her horse and they began riding after Brock.

"I hope he's not going to be like this the whole time," said Brittany.

CHAPTER 7
Not As Expected

I just don't like it," exclaimed Shank. He looked around uneasily at the desert, the ocean and the forces of the House of Hiram. "I just don't like it."

"What are you thinking," asked Reed?

"It's too easy," answered Herald and Shank at the same time.

Reed nodded his head.

"I agree," he said, "This is not what I expected."

As the armies of the House of Hiram marched closer to the harbor, Lords Reed, Shank and Herald became more and more suspicious.

"Why are we worried?" asked Reed. "They can't outflank us," he declared. "On our right is the desert and on our left is the sea."

All three subconsciously looked out at the ocean. They could see *Vengeance* and *Scorpion* sailing along the horizon. The rest of the fleet was rushing toward the harbor.

"Norrom owns the sea," said Reed confidently. "There is little threat there."

Shank and Herald nodded in agreement.

"My men patrol our right flank deep into the desert," said Reed. "They assure me they can see for miles and no one is out there."

"Our rear is guarded by the lancers," added Shank.

"And I have some Greens following from behind as well," said Reed with a smile.

Shank and Herald laughed.

"We can always count on you, Reed," said Herald. His smile was full and bright.

"The Greens report there is a palace-fortress," said Reed, quietly, "with much activity."

"So, they know we are here," said Herald, speaking the obvious.

"We know one rider made it past our arrows," said Shank, unhappily. "We know he made it to the tower; we can see the smoke."

"So, they know we are here," said Herald, again. "If we can see the signal fire, they can see the signal fire."

"What's your point?" asked Reed.

"They know we are here," said Herald, "yet they do nothing to stop us. They offer no resistance at all. This is not what I expected."

The forces of the House of Hiram marched on. As they crested a hill, Reed raised his hand to stop.

Before them was a road leading downward right to the city itself. The road was totally unguarded, totally empty. They could see the seawall, the harbor and the city gates.

At the city gates fisherman and merchants rushed to get within the city walls, yet the gates remained opened and unguarded.

In the harbor itself a number of Porco warships stayed at anchor; all unmanned and unguarded, or so it seemed.

On the seawall, the tower blazed mightily, but the door to the tower was open and unguarded.

"Look," shouted Herald. "*Tempest* is moving. He pointed to the harbor. "Ram is opening the mouth of the harbor for the rest of the fleet."

Ships of the House of Hiram sailed into the harbor unopposed.

"It looks like *Fyrmatus* is headed for *The Black Claw*," cried Shank.

The three watched Falcon's ship with growing anticipation.

"Fyrmatus is going to dock right next to *The Black Claw,"* shouted Shank.

"Forward," commanded Lord Reed. "Hurry!" he cried. "Let's see if we can beat Falcon into the city."

His words were significantly lighter than his heart.

The main invasion force of the House of Hiram ran toward the city with a great shout. In the distance, *Fyrmatus* docked next to *The Black Claw*.

"Tie those lines," shouted Mr. Schooper as *Fyrmatus* moved in to share the opposite side of the dock with *The Black Claw*.

"Secure that ship," commanded Falcon, even before *Fyrmatus* had stopped moving.

Instantly, men in red uniforms swarmed across the dock and onto *The Black Claw*.

The men quickly and carefully moved through the four decks of this horrid slave ship.

The main deck was obviously empty, but every inch was searched, nonetheless.

"Main deck secured, sir" shouted one of the Reds; an officer name Halston.

The second deck, where the crew slept, was likewise secured. It was lined with rows of hammocks, hung one above the other, three high. The stench of sweat and filth in this deck made some of the Reds gag and retch.

"Second deck secured, sir" shouted Halston.

The Reds moved slowly through the third deck. It was where the slave oarsmen lived and worked and died.

This deck was built to house at least 100 men to work the oars. Chains and shackles still lay on the floor marred by bits of rotting flesh and dried blood.

Halston's voice was heard shouting to Falcon. "Third deck secured, sir!"

The fourth deck was the foulest of all. It was built to hold row upon row of human cargo. The slaves would normally be chained and packed so densely that they could barely move.

This deck on *The Black Claw*, however, had been modified. There were no chains. Instead silk tents were attached to the beams above and hung all the way down to the floor. Each tent was intended to house one kidnapped girl, taken for the pleasure of the late Prince Rhala'nn.

The Reds moved carefully through the last deck. They cautiously ripped open each of the tents to reveal silken cushions and blankets, but no victims.

When fully searched, the Reds hurried back up to daylight and fresh air. The hatches were locked so that no guard needed to remain below.

"Sir," shouted Halston. *The Black Claw* is secure. No one was onboard."

"Very good," replied Lord Falcon in a loud confident voice.

More quietly he asked, "Was there any evidence that Lady Cilantra had been onboard?"

The confidence in his voice was replaced by a fear-tinted hope.

Halston lowered his eyes and shook his head. "No sir," he said simply.

While the squad of Reds was searching *The Black Claw,* Falcon had ordered others from his ship to take the city gates.

Here, he expected resistance, but there was none. Within minutes the Reds poured through the main gates of Saalespor.

Panicked Porco ran from their shops and stalls. Mothers scooped up their children and ran screaming up the main street. Apartments were abandoned, windows shuttered and doors locked.

Falcon's men carefully searched the shops that were built in and around the city walls. They all seemed to have been abandoned within the last hour. In one shop, mugs of tea were found sitting on a table, still warm; half eaten plates of food were nearby.

Lord Reed and the main invasion force were just passing the seawall when the first of the Reds entered the city.

Reed smiled as he saw the Reds run through the gates.

Next time, he said to himself. *We'll be first next time.*

He knew it was not true. The Reds were always the first into battle and usually the first to shed blood.

As the city gates fell, *Celantra* dropped anchor in the center of the harbor. From this advantage point, Herald's men could easily signal all the other ships. *Sea Core* dropped anchor next to *Celantra*. In so doing, Lord Norrom kept his flag ship at the center of action.

The captains of *Gauntlet,* *Advocate,* *Adventurer and Valiant* easily found empty docks on which to moor their ships.

"This has got to be the easiest invasion of all time," said Tulmar as he stepped onto the dock. Pausing, he added, "This is not what I expected; but, then again, it's not over yet."

ය   ය   ය   ය   ය

The farther along the road Brock, Cilantra and Brittany traveled the faster they wanted the horses to run. At first they started slowly, worried about being heard and seen. Now, they ignored all caution and galloped recklessly along the road. Having just passed the kitchen area, Brock knew they would soon reach the alley that led to the main road. He slowed his horse to a walk. Cilantra and Brittany did likewise.

"Listen, began Brock." We should come to a dark little alley soon"

"You mean the one that leads to the guard shack and the big iron gates," asked Brittany?

How do you know about that, thought Brock? But what his mouth said was, "Yes, exactly."

"I'm not sure what we are going to tell the guards" began Brock, "but we have to get through those gates.

His voice was full of confidence even if his heart was not.

Suddenly, there came shouted voices from ahead. Brock, Cilantra and Brittany pulled their horses to a stop and froze in their saddles.

Brock motioned with his hand.

"Stay here," he whispered.

The horses' ears moved forward and back and forward again. Their tails switched nervously.

Brock lightly kicked his horse and slowly moved forward. From around a bend in the road Brock watched as four royal guards ran wildly out of the Woman's Garden and down the alley.

He carefully looked through the opening to the Woman's Garden. All was calm and green and beautiful. Brock turned his horse and walked back to where Cilantra and Brittany were waiting.

"I don't know for sure," he said "but I think they may have discovered you are missing."

He quietly described what he saw.

"We have to keep going," said Cilantra with confidence. "If they know we are trying to escape, going back is the last thing we should do.

If they don't know, then we should also keep going."

Brittany nodded silently.

"Are you ready?" Brock asked.

Even though they were frightened, they both nodded their heads.

Brock, Cilantra and Brittany slowly and carefully rode up to the opening to the Woman's Garden. All was as it should be.

They quietly moved forward into the alley.

The ride down the alley was the longest and darkest ride the three had ever taken. Every little sound or shadow caused them to jump; leaves swirling in the wind, a rat scurrying in the shadows, everything. Even the horses seemed tense and alert.

Finally, up ahead, they could see the bright light of day coming from the street.

Brock was about to say, "You wait here and let me see about the guards," when there came a great clamor from behind.

"Hurry," shouted Brock. "Someone is coming!"

With that he kicked his horse and ran madly toward the gate. Cilantra and Brittany followed fast behind him.

Try as he might, he could not think of a plan to get the guards to open the gate.

I'll just have to fight them, he thought, finally. He ignored the fact that with the four guards he had seen running down the alley and the two at the shack, he would have to fight at least six Porco guards.

The closer he got to the guard shack and the gate, however, the more it looked like the guards were gone and the gates were open.

He could see clusters of people running past the gate, up the road away from the harbor. There was no trace of the guards, and the gates were, indeed, wide open.

"This is not what I expected," he said to himself.

A cacophony of shouts and frightened voices erupted from behind.

"Hurry," shouted Brock. "Just follow me!"

He kicked his horse and galloped full-speed through the gates. Brock galloped across the main road without pausing to look up or down it. Cilantra and Brittany followed right behind. When he reached the other side of the road Brock turned and rode a few yards toward the harbor.

The road was full of panicked people streaming up from the lower sections of the city. Brock rode boldly into the mass of frightened Porco. So intent were they to continue their escape that the Porco simply ran around the horses and continued up the road.

They want to escape as much as we do, thought Brock.

In moments, Brock found a familiar lane. At the intersection of the lane and the main road was a round, two-tiered fountain. A stone angel at the top of the fountain dribbled water from its mouth. It was covered in green moss and looked odd.

Brock let the horses drink a little. He then led Cilantra and Brittany up the lane into a secluded neighborhood of large and now, deserted houses.

The stillness of the lane was a welcome relief.

"What has happened," asked Brittany?

"I thought at first they were looking for us," replied Cilantra, "but that can't be right."

"I don't know," said Brock, "but it couldn't be better for us."

He listened carefully.

"All this confusion will mask our escape," he said with a nervous laugh. "No one will remember seeing us."

"What should we do now," asked Brittany?

She was thankful just to be out of the palace.

"I know a way to get from here into the desert," Brock replied. "I have been living there in a cave," he said with a smile. "We can hide in the cave until we find out what is going on."

"What about the horses?" asked Cilantra.

"They can hide with us," answered Brock. "The caves are huge. There is even a fresh water spring. With fish from the sea for food, we could stay there for the rest of our lives."

"Let's hope it doesn't come to that," said Cilantra, with a funny smile.

"I think we should go now," said Brittany, suddenly. "Listen."

"What is it," asked Cilantra?

"I don't hear anything," added Brock.

"Exactly," said Brittany. "Everything is quiet. The main road sounds deserted."

Everyone stopped and listened. There was not a sound.

"I don't want to find out what they were all running from," said Brittany, her voice tinged with fear.

"We should go to the caves," said Cilantra.

Without another word, Brock turned his horse and started trotting up the lane. Cilantra and Brittany followed. They passed one huge house after another, all enclosed by walls, all surrounded by lush gardens and all abandoned.

In a short time, the houses gave way to open land which then faded into hilly desert.

Brock stopped and gazed toward the city.

"Look!" he shouted.

Pointing toward the harbor he yelled, "There's smoke. The tower is burning. We have to hide; hurry!"

He kicked his horse into a run. Cilantra and Brittany followed as he led them onto an almost undetectable path. It opened onto a trail between two high hills. The trail was dotted with green shrubs and lush trees.

"This is what led me to the caves," explained Brock. "I figured these green plants had to have a source of water. When I found the water, it led me to the caves."

Brock stopped his horse and dismounted. "We have to walk from here," he explained.

Taking his horse by the reigns, Brock led them off the trail through dense brush.

"There is plenty here for the horses to eat," said Cilantra. She was having a little trouble leading her horse.

"And drink, I imagine," added Brittany. She had noticed a trickle of water flowing downhill through this hidden canyon.

Brock was leading them up a steep hill when suddenly he disappeared.

"Where did he go?" asked Brittany with a nervous laugh.

"He was right there, a moment ago," said Cilantra, pointing to the spot Brock and his horse had been.

"Brock, where are you?" they shouted.

The sound of laughter came from behind a large bolder. Brock stepped out from behind the rock. He was pleased his little trick had worked.

"Right this way, ladies," said Brock laughing loudly. His voice echoed noisily throughout the little hidden canyon.

He led them around the bolder and through an opening in the rocky hillside. They had to walk the horses single file through the opening. It was barely big enough for the horses.

"This is not what I expected," said Brittany.

The little mouth of the cave opened into a huge cavern. It was cool inside and dark, except for shafts of sunlight beaming down from high above. The sound of trickling water could be heard coming from within the cave.

"Welcome to my humble home," said Brock, lightly.

Outside in the distance, two men heard a man's laugh echoing loudly through the canyon. They glanced at one another, then without a word, began moving quickly toward the sound.

ﻼ   ﻼ   ﻼ   ﻼ   ﻼ

Falcon left *Frymatus* and ran to the city gates just as Reed, Shank and Herald arrived.

"Anything?" asked Falcon, as he hugged his brothers.

They all shook their heads.

"We haven't seen any form of defense. There has been no resistance at all?" said Reed.

Falcon frowned, slightly.

"We haven't seen any sign of Cilantra or Brittany either," added Reed when he realized Falcon's question was more personal than professional.

Shank looked at a group of Yellows entering the city gates. He stepped toward them.

"Secure the walls," shouted Shank.

In moments, Yellows swarmed up ladders and stairways to the top of the city walls. From the walls they could see both the harbor and the inside of the city. The Yellows alternated their stance so that half faced outside while the other half faced inside. The archers thus guarded against an attack from outside the city and from within.

Shortly, a runner approached Shank and briefly spoke with him.

"My men report there is a palace-fortress manned by substantial forces," said Reed. "I think the whole city has taken refuge there."

"Falcon," declared Shank rather loudly. "My men have taken the city walls." Then, in a lower voice he reported, "There was one injury, but he will live."

Falcon, Reed and Herald all looked at Shank in alarm.

"Finally, battle!" said Falcon.

Shank shook his head, sheepishly.

"No," he said, quietly. "One of my men was running up the stairs to the top of the walls," said Shank. "He tripped and rammed the arrow he was holding into his own leg."

Falcon, Reed and Herald all burst out laughing.

"Please don't tell me who it is," begged Falcon. "I don't want to know his name," he added, smiling broadly.

"They're already calling him *Ram Junior*," said Shank.

Reed and Herald laughed all the harder.

Falcon shook his head and then returned to the business at hand.

"Please signal *Tempest*," commanded Falcon. "Tell Ram to start bringing his war machines into the city."

"Of course," replied Herald.

"And signal *Vengeance*," continued Falcon. "Tell Father we may need to introduce the Porco to Gannon's special passenger sooner than expected."

"As you wish," replied Herald, respectfully.

"Reed," continued Falcon, "Ram needs to know everything your men have learned about the palace-fortress. He'll want to choose just the right machines for the attack."

"Of course," replied Reed.

"Shank," said Falcon.

"Yes, brother," replied Shank, still a little embarrassed.

"Leave a few men on the wall," said Falcon; "however many you think is prudent."

Shank nodded. "Understood," he replied. "The rest will be needed at the palace-fortress."

"Exactly,' said Falcon with a smile.

"And Shank," he added. "Tell *Ram Junior* that the pointy part of the arrow goes into the bad guys, not the good guys."

Reed, Herald and Shank laughed loudly.

"I think he has learned that all by himself," replied Shank.

"That's good to hear," said Falcon, smiling.

"Herald," said Falcon; "One more thing. "Please signal the Lancers. I want them here, now."

"Of course," replied Herald.

Falcon watched proudly as members of The Reds fanned out through the stores, stalls and apartments that were near the city wall. Nothing would be left unchecked.

"I need Halston here," shouted Falcon; "with twenty of his best men."

A runner immediately left for *Frymatus.*

Within a few minutes, the ground began to shake with the thundering sound of galloping horses. They came, three abreast, through the city gates. Behind the Lancers ran Halston and twenty of his best men.

"Lancers, reporting as ordered," shouted Gibson, the lead Lancer. Falcon acknowledged Halston with a nod, and then looked at Gibson.

"Very good," said Falcon. "I want the Lancers to ride as far as they can up the main road. Make sure the Porco are not in hiding, waiting to attack us. If you find them, do not engage them. Just return here and tell us where they are."

"Understood," replied Gibson.

"There is a palace-fortress at the top of the main road. Do not approach it. I just want to know how far up the main road our troops can go before we engage the enemy."

"Understood," replied Gibson, again.

Gibson motioned to one of his officers named Karson, and issued his commands. The man was soon riding up the main road with the first wave of cavalry.

"One more thing, Gibson," shouted Falcon loudly.

The sound of horses and men made it almost impossible to be heard.

"I need twenty-one of your best horsemen for another mission," said Falcon. "An important mission," he added, unnecessarily.

"Yes, sir," replied Gibson, smartly.

Pointing to Halston, Falcon continued.

"He and twenty other Reds will ride with twenty-one of your Silvers," explained Falcon.

Gibson, Halston and twenty Reds listened as carefully as they could.

"Lady Cilantra and her friend Brittany have been kidnapped," said Falcon.

Just speaking the words aloud brought fire to his heart.

"They are being held somewhere in this miserable rat-hole of a city," exclaimed Falcon, angrily. "They could be anywhere."

He paused for a moment to regain his composure.

"I want you to find them," said Falcon simply; "and if you can, rescue them."

"It will be an honor, sir," replied Halston.

As he spoke, a pair of riders crowded their way into the group.

Falcon smiled. "I've been wondering when I'd see you," he said, happily.

Quasar and Nemo smiled, holding their horses firmly in check.

"I don't ever want to know how you got those horses," said Falcon with a smile.

"Don't forget about Brock," said Quasar. He was in no mood to smile.

He wanted to say, '*What are you doing to find Brittany*,' but Nemo knew Falcon was as worried about his own wife as he was about Brittany.

"Brock is a good man," added Nemo.

"I've been wondering about Brock," said Falcon. "Are you sure he wasn't lost at sea?" he asked, gently.

"He's here," said Quasar, firmly. "I know he is."

"All ears, all eyes to me," cried Falcon, loudly.

Everyone within earshot stopped what they were doing and turned to Falcon.

"Lady Cilantra and Brittany are somewhere in this rat's nest," exclaimed Falcon. "So is a good man named Brock, who came here to help them. We have not heard from Brock since the storm."

"This is Nemo, Lord of Silverglade, and Quasar, the Dragon-Slayer," he continued, pointing to his friends. "Quasar is Brittany's husband."

"Most of you know Quasar and Nemo already," said Falcon. "Follow their commands as if they were my own."

ʊ҆ ʊ҆ ʊ҆ ʊ҆ ʊ҆

King Ahala'nn gazed down from the upper walls of his palace. Far below, he could see masses of his people crowding before the palace gates. Their cries for help echoed up the stone walls, even to the King's ears.

"General Ryguy Roces," cried the King.

"Your Majesty," replied the general as he ran to King Ahala'nn's side.

"Open the gates," ordered the King. "The city has come to me for protection."

"As you wish, Your Majesty," replied the general. "But," he said with deference. "There is just one thing."

"Speak freely, Ryguy," said the King. "You are now the closest thing I have to a son," said the King, sadly.

"As you know," began the general, "there are warships in the harbor and a large force has entered the city."

"And you would warn me," interrupted the King, "that if I open the gates for the people, I may well be opening the gates for the invaders."

"Yes, Your Majesty," replied the general.

"I have too long ignored the needs of Saalespor," confessed the King; "But I still have time to right many wrongs."

"Open the gates, Ryguy" ordered the King.

"Yes, Your Majesty," replied the general.

"One more thing, Ryguy?" asked the King.

"Yes, Your Majesty," replied the general.

He was not accustomed to the King calling him by his first name.

This is not what I expected, he thought. *What should I do?*

Serve your king no matter what you expected, replied his own mind. *He needs you more now than ever.*

"Where is the Navy, Ryguy?" asked the King. "Why have these warships entered our harbor unchallenged? Why have troops landed unopposed?"

"The Navy, sir?" asked the general. He was trying to think of an acceptable answer.

"I know that Prince Rhala'nn named himself *Admiral of the Navy*," admitted the King. "But I have many loyal Captains. Where are the ships?"

"Your Majesty," began the general. "The Admiral Prince Rhala'nn ordered the Navy to escort a large flotilla to the marketplace."

"What marketplace?" asked the bewildered King. "It is not the time to sell silk."

"Not the silk marketplace," replied the general; "the slave marketplace."

"What slaves?" cried the King in anguish.

The general took a deep breath, vying for time and an acceptable answer.

Truth is always the best answer, he told himself.

"While his Spotters and Takers were kidnapping 'Favored Ones," explained the general, "Prince Rhala'nn used the army to capture slaves."

"Slaves?" cried the King. "I ended slave trade," declared the King.

"Yes, Your Majesty," replied the general, "but the Prince resumed it."

The King looked bewildered. He had long been uninterested in the daily affairs of Saalespor. This vacuum of power was filled by corruption and evil.

"This is not what I expected," said the King. His voice rang with guilt.

"More than half our men are gone on raiding parties, ordered by the Prince," explained the general. His voice was filled with sadness and anger.

At this news, all color drained from the King's face; he collected himself as much as possible.

"See to the gates, General," said the King, quietly. "Let as many in as you possibly can. If any can fight, send them to the armory."

"Yes, Your Majesty," replied the general.

He left the King leaning feebly against the upper fortress wall.

"What have you done, my son?" cried the King. "Half the army is enslaving the innocent and the Navy is selling them at market!"

"What have you done, my son?" repeated the King.

"What have I done?" asked the King in a moment of clarity.

"How can I defend my kingdom?"

Far in the distance, the King watched as a group of silver Lancers carefully made their way up the main road.

As the palace-fortress came into view, Karson stopped his men and ordered them to dismount.

Looking ahead to the palace-fortress, Karson shook his head in disbelief.

"This is not what I expected," he said to no one in particular.

Karson motioned to a horseman and ordered him to ride to Falcon with good news:

"No resistance on the main road. The palace gates are open."

❧   ❧   ❧   ❧   ❧

Quasar rode up the main street with reckless abandon. For as good a rider as he was, Nemo still had a hard time keeping up with Quasar.

Halston and the Reds followed in three columns of seven, sharing horses with twenty-one Lancers. They all rode with the speed of a battle charge. As far as Quasar was concerned, they were in a battle to save Brittany's life.

Suddenly, without signaling the Lancers behind him, Quasar pulled his horse hard left and brought her to a rapid stop. Only the excellent horsemanship of the Lancers avoided a deadly crash in a cloud of dust.

Gibson shouted a command and signaled with his right hand. Instantly, all three columns veered right, barley missing Quasar. The Lancers pulled each of their horses in a tight half-circle. The three columns stopped facing the opposite direction. It was a well-practiced maneuver which may have saved their lives.

Nemo was the last to react. Rapidly turning his horse, he barely kept his seat. As the dust began to settle, Nemo rode directly to Quasar and stopped.

"What are you doing?" he shouted.

Nemo was both annoyed and frightened. Adrenaline rushed through his veins. His heart pounded in his throat.

Quasar looked at his friend; the fire of battle in his eyes.

"The gate is open," said Quasar, hotly.

"And for that we should all die?" asked Nemo, sarcastically.

"There is a guard shack, but no guards," said Quasar, as if that answered all questions.

"Do any of you know what's down there?" asked Nemo, pointing at the shadowy alley.

All the Lancers and the Reds shook their heads.

"I want to go down there," said Quasar, looking as far into the alley as he could see.

"We'll all go with you," replied Nemo

He tried to speak kindly to his friend even though he was still angry.

"It's too narrow for three columns of horses," said Quasar, still looking down the alley.

"Then we'll go in single file," answered Nemo.

"One column will follow me into the alley," commanded Quasar in a loud voice

Without waiting for anyone or anything, Quasar kicked his horse and rode rapidly through the iron gates.

Nemo's mouth dropped open. He had never seen Quasar act like this.

"Gibson," cried Nemo. "We would like a column to accompany us down this alley."

"Yes, sir," replied Gibson.

With a mere wave of his hand, a column of seven Lancers with their seven saddle-mate Reds rode off behind Quasar.

Gibson was none too happy about the way Quasar had recklessly risked their lives.

My job is not about being happy, Gibson reminded himself. *My job is to follow their orders as if they came from Lord Falcon himself.*

"Water your horses, Gibson; if you'd like," suggested Nemo.

"Very good," replied Gibson.

A few yards from where they stood was a round two-tiered fountain. At its top, water dribbled from the mouth of a moss covered stone angel.

"We will meet you there," said Nemo, pointing to the fountain; "or we will send word if we find anything."

"As you wish," replied Gibson.

"Make sure the streets and lanes around here do not hide Porco, waiting to attack," added Nemo.

He did not need to tell Gibson how to do his job.

"Of course," replied Gibson.

As Nemo watched, Quasar and the seven Lancers disappeared into the darkness of the alley ahead. Nemo turned his horse and sprinted through the gates. He would have to ride fast if he hoped to catch up with the column.

ᘓ ᘓ ᘓ ᘓ ᘓ

The road to the main gates of the palace-fortress was littered with abandoned carts, discarded sacks and all manner of personal belongings jettisoned in panic.

The steep lane that led down from the fortress gates to the main road was crowded with the last refugees from the city. Women cried, children wailed, the old and infirm were pushed aside in a mad rush for sanctuary. Chaos was the norm.

General Ryguy Roces rode slowly through the anarchy of the Common Courtyard. It was crowded with desperate people and filled with the stench of fear. He stopped at the scaffold built in the center of the courtyard.

Hanging by his wrists was a shirtless man covered in sweat from pain and the hot desert sun. He had been there since early morning.

Large bags filled with sand hung from his ankles, legs, knees and waist. He dangled from the scaffold in agony; the weight of the bags pulling cruelly on his joints and lungs.

The man opened one eye and looked at General Ryguy Roces.

"It is good to see you again, General," said the man. He coughed and gagged at the effort.

"Do I know you?" asked the general.

The man's features were so grotesquely twisted in pain that he was unrecognizable.

"I am Treanor," said the man, weakly. "I served under you."

"Ah yes," replied General Ryguy Roces, sadly; "until you accepted a promotion to serve the Prince."

"Captain of his personal guard," said the man, proudly.

"How then do you find yourself here?" asked the general. He well knew the answer.

"The Prince acted wickedly," answered Treanor.

"So did you," said the general, dryly.

"I was only following orders," explained Treanor.

"That excuse has been used since the beginning of time," said the general; "and always by those who did evil."

The general looked sadly at the man.

"We are all responsible for what we do," proclaimed the general.

"Had I not followed orders, I would have paid with pain," argued Treanor.

"You are paying with pain, anyway," said the general; his voice filled with gloom.

"True," agreed Treanor; wheezing a twisted laugh.

"To pay with pain for being honorable is one thing," explained the general. "To pay with pain for being wicked is another thing altogether," he concluded.

"True," agreed Treanor, again. This time he did not laugh.

"General, please" begged Treanor; "One favor."

General Ryguy Roces sat on his horse in silence, deaf to the roar of the crowd around him. He eyed the man in pity.

"What?" he asked.

"Kill me," begged Treanor. "If ever I served you well, kill me."

"You served me well, but you chose poorly," answered the general. He moved his horse close the ill-fated man.

With one sudden swift motion, General Ryguy Roces drew his sword and brought it down in a perfect arch.

Treanor squeezed his eyes shut and waited, thankfully, for death.

The blade cut one sack after another. Sand poured out, slowly lessening the tortious pull on joints and lungs.

As Treanor began to breathe normally, he opened his eyes.

"This is not what I expected," he moaned.

"You once served me well," said the general. "Now live again," he exclaimed, "and live honorably!"

With one more swipe of his blade, the general cut the bonds that tied Treanor's wrists to the crossbeam. His joints screamed in protest as he landed hard on the dirt below.

"Get yourself to the healers," said General Ryguy Roces.

"Remember, Treanor," said the general as he turned his horse. "Few are given life anew. Live well, live true."

General Ryguy Roces kicked his horse forward through the teaming throng.

He frowned at sight of the guards manning the gates. They had lost control of everything.

"Prepare to close these gates," shouted the general.

The sound of his voice shocked the guards, who had not seen him ride up. They snapped at attention but said nothing.

"Did you hear me?" barked the general.

"Yes sir," replied all six guards in unison.

One brave man stepped forward.

"Forgive me, General," he began. "The people are swarming everywhere," he said, alarm ringing in his voice. "How can we close the gates without crushing them?"

"You four," cried the general, angrily, "start pushing the left gate closed. The people will hurry through the open the right side."

"You two," shouted the general, pointing to the man who had dared speak and the one next to him.

"Clear this courtyard," snarled the general. "Send those who can fight to the armory. Get the rest to the Great Hall or the Upper Courtyard."

"Yes sir," they both replied.

"One last thing," shouted the general over the roar of the crowd.

"Do you see that man?" he asked.

The general pointed to the motionless heap at the foot of the scaffold.

"Treanor?" asked the man who had spoken.

"Yes," replied the general. "Get him to the healers."

"Yes sir," they both replied, again.

The general walked his horse carefully through the throng crowding its way into the palace-fortress.

He stopped outside the gates and looked down the steep lane that led to the main road. People filled the lane; running, pushing, fighting to get up the steep grade.

The last two refugees struggled at the bottom of the lane. An old man, barely strong enough to make the ascent himself was trying to bring a frail old woman with him.

In the distance, the general noticed four men dressed in green appear on the main road and then disappear again.

The enemy is upon us, thought General Ryguy Roces. Shaking his head slowly he said to himself, "This is not what I expected."

Kicking his horse, the general made his way toward the old couple.

A roar went up from the crowd as they saw the left gate beginning to close. The throng quickened its way into the palace-fortress.

General Ryguy Roces stopped his horse.

"Can you get on my horse, old man?" asked the general. His voice was surprisingly gentle.

The old man looked in the direction of the voice. His milky eyes could barely make out the figure of a man upon a horse.

He shook his head and spoke firmly.

"Not without my wife!"

General Ryguy Roces smiled and dismounted.

"I wish I had a thousand like you," said the general, tenderly. "Honor is a rare thing these days."

"A little younger, perhaps," said the old man.

The general laughed aloud.

"Yes, a thousand like you, but perhaps a little younger," he admitted.

"Up with you now," said the general, helping the old man into the saddle. "I'll not leave your wife," he promised.

The old man, who was unexpectedly spry, got himself onto the warhorse. With his help, the general succeeded in getting the old woman onto the horse as well. She smiled a toothless grin.

"Thank you, sir," she said humbly.

The sound of horse and rider shocked the general from this brief interval with humanity.

"What is it?" shouted the general, even before the rider had stopped.

The man respectfully dismounted. It would not do for a messenger to look down upon a general.

"Sir," replied the rider. "It is your brother."

A dark cloud of pain descended upon General Ryguy Roces.

"What news?" asked the general, quietly. He knew in the Upper Courtyard that his brother would die.

"Captain Hacim Roces," announced the messenger, formally, "is asking for you."

"What?" shouted the general.

He could not hope to believe the words he had heard.

"Your brother lives," said the messenger, urgently. "He is asking for you. He says he has critical information for your ears alone."

General Ryguy Roces grabbed the reigns of the messenger's horse and gave him the reigns of his own horse.

"See to the safety of this old couple," ordered the general, as he mounted the messenger's horse.

"Treat them as you would your own family," he added.

Without a moment's delay, the general galloped toward the palace-fortress.

"As you wish, General," replied the messenger. He had not bothered to even look at the couple sitting upon the general's horse.

"Son?" asked the old man. "Is that your voice I hear?"

The messenger gazed at the old man in disbelief.

"Father, Mother," he cried as disbelief gave way to amazement.

"I was so worried about you," said the messenger and his mother at the same time.

Tears flowed from the messenger's eyes and the unseeing eyes of the old man, but a frown creased the old woman's face.

"They've not been feeding you enough," she said, gazing at her last born. "You're all bone!"

"I'm fine," laughed the messenger. He reached up and touched her face tenderly.

"Let's get you to safety," he said with a smile.

With that, the messenger ran up the steep lane that led to the main fortress gates, pulling the horse and riders behind him.

The gates were shut moments after they came through.

"Thank you for waiting," said the old woman to the guards.

"Get as far inside as you can," said one of the guards. "They're here!"

On the main road, just beyond an arrow's reach, a cluster of soldiers dressed in green watched the gates close.

Behind them, a phalanx of Lancers assembled four deep across the road.

ଓ   ଓ   ଓ   ଓ   ଓ

Quasar and Nemo gazed from the alley into the Woman's Garden.

"This is not what I expected," said Nemo.

"It reminds me a little of Silverglade," said Quasar.

"It's nice, but it's nothing like Silverglade," replied Nemo.

Just the mention of his enchanted valley brought joy to Nemo's heart, short lived as it was.

"Do you think Brittany and Cilantra might be in there?" he asked.

"They might," said Quasar. Fire smoldered behind his eyes.

As Quasar dismounted, Nemo and the seven Reds behind him did likewise. Quasar turned to the Lancers.

"Ride down this road," he ordered. "See what there is to see, then meet us back here."

The column immediately rode off down the alley road.

"Halston," said Quasar. "Let's see how fruitful this garden is."

Halston and the six other Reds slipped into the Woman's Garden. Quasar and Nemo left their horses at the edge of alley and followed the Reds through the opening in the wall.

"We want to be as quiet as we can," whispered Quasar. He spoke to himself as much as to anyone else.

The garden was as silent as a cemetery. The only sound the men could hear was of splashing water from some distant fountain. The nine moved slowly and cautiously from the alley and fanned out across a well-kept lawn.

"There is something wrong here," whispered Quasar as he walked down a wide garden path.

The beauty of the garden was marred by arbitrary items seemingly discarded at random; a shoe, a doll, a sack of food. These things were out of place in this perfectly manicured garden.

Nemo bent down and retrieved a bit of cloth that had little bells sewn onto it.

"This is the torn hem of a child's dress," said Nemo, examining it closely.

"What happened here," he wondered aloud?

Nemo tossed the cloth aside. It made a sharp tinkling sound as it flew through the air.

Hidden deep within the shrubbery of a flowering archway two eyes watched as the nine made their way through the garden.

Quasar, Nemo and the Reds stopped at the sight of the palace portico. The remnant of bedlam was seen everywhere. Plants were trampled, furniture was overturned. Life's precious mementoes were tossed out like yesterday's fish heads.

"What happened here?" asked Nemo again.

He was answered by the sound of a horse galloping through the garden. The sound of steal rang out as the Reds drew their swords. Suddenly, a horse jumped a low hedge and came to rest near Quasar and Nemo.

"Sir," cried the Lancer, as he dismounted. "The palace seems deserted."

He stepped closer to Quasar and continued.

"We found two dead guards in the dirt, on the perimeter road; not long dead. And there are footprints in the dirt."

"Footprints?" asked Quasar.

"Yes sir, footprints," replied the Lancer as he caught his breath.

"One man and two women," he continued. "It looks like they left riding two horses.

Quasar and Nemo looked at one another and smiled.

"Brittany and Cilantra," said Quasar.

He dared not fully hope.

"And Brock! added Nemo.

Quasar stood as if cast in stone. The news flooded his mind with a thousand thoughts.

"Is there anything else?" asked Nemo.

The Lancer reached his hand out toward Nemo.

"Only this," he said, handing Nemo a thin white ribbon decorated by tiny embroidered flowers.

"Where did you get that?" shouted Quasar. He snatched the ribbon from Nemo.

A downpour of emotions rained over Quasar.

"This is Brittany's!" he cried. "She left it for me on the forest road. I gave it to Brock. He must have given it to her."

"Where did you get this?" asked Quasar. He was barely able to contain his excitement.

"It was in the dirt," answered the Lancer. He didn't want to again mention the two dead guards.

"In the dirt?" repeated Quasar. "With the guards?" he asked; "with the two dead guards?"

"Yes sir," replied the Lancer; "With the guards and the footprints; one man, two women and horses."

"They're alive! cried Quasar. "Brittany, Cilantra and Brock are alive!"

He embraced Nemo so hard they almost fell over.

The Reds cheered. Quasar patted the Lancer on his back and hugged Halston.

"They're alive!" said Quasar again!

From within the low hedge a set of eyes saw all they needed to see.

CHAPTER 8
The Meeting

*T*he doors of the healing hall burst open as General Ryguy Roces rushed in.

A man dressed in the white flowing robes of a healer hurried to him.

"You must be..." began the healer.

"Where is he?" interrupted the general.

He looked quickly around the hall. It was virtually empty except for others dressed in white. They were all busy preparing for the anticipated onslaught to come.

"General," replied the man in a calm soothing voice. "Whom do you seek?"

"My brother, of course," replied the general impatiently.

"Of course," replied the healer. "That would be Hacim."

"Captain Hacim Roces," said the general, firmly.

"Your brother is strong of will," said the healer. *It must run in the family*, he thought.

"He fends off death, waiting to speak to you," explained the healer. "It may be all that's keeping him alive."

"But he will live," said the general.

"I'm a healer, not an oracle," replied the man. "Walk with me," he said and moved briskly from the hall.

The healer led the general to a private alcove off of the main hall. Hacim Roces was lying on a mat, gray with death. A young woman knelt next to him, wiping his head with a moist cloth.

"How is he?" asked the healer.

"We have tended his wounds," said the woman. "He no longer bleeds."

"This is General Ryguy Roces," said the healer.

"Your brother has been asking for you," said the woman as she stood.

She returned the moist cloth to a shallow bowl that rested on a nearby table, and then dried her hands. Turning to the general, she took his hands gently into her own.

"He loves you," she said tenderly. "It is a powerful thing."

The woman released the general's hands and nodded respectfully to the healer. She then walked silently from the alcove. The healer followed her.

General Ryguy Roces knelt next to his brother.

"Hacim," he said quietly, "I'm here."

The general smiled broadly when his brother opened his eyes.

"Ryguy," said Captain Hacim Roces, weakly. "I have so much to tell you."

ೞ ೞ ೞ ೞ ೞ

Reed ran breathlessly to his brother with the news.

"Falcon," he cried. "The Greens report the city is ours. The Porco have all fled to the palace-fortress."

From the top of the city walls, Falcon and Reed surveyed the empty buildings and roads of Saalespor. Only forces loyal to the House of Hiram could be seen.

In the harbor, *Tempest* again prepared to strike the tower.

"Release," shouted Ram.

A single boulder flew from the ship.

"Yes," cried Ram, as his mind calculated the arc of the flying stone.

The boulder crashed into the top of the tower exploding it like a blast of thunder.

Falcon and Reed turned toward the sound.

They watched as burning wood and charred blocks rained down upon the seawall. The water below erupted with falling debris.

On *Tempest*, Ram screamed "Yes!" again, and pumped his fist in the air.

Falcon and Reed looked at one another. "Yes!" they shouted, and all but danced with joy on the city wall.

"They'll be no living with him, now," laughed Reed. "I was never sure about sailing on a ship filled with heavy rocks."

"Ram always said, 'cargo is cargo'," quoted Falcon.

"They'll just be no living with him, now," Reed said again.

"Herald!" shouted Falcon waving his arms.

"I saw," shouted Herald, as he ran along the wall to his brothers. He was as excited as they were.

"Send a message to *Tempest*," said Falcon as Herald arrived. "I want those machines at the fortress, now!"

"As you wish," replied Herald.

"And signal *Vengeance* and *Scorpion*." He added. "Tell them it's time."

In mere seconds, light flashed from the city walls to the ships on the horizon, then back again from the ships to the city walls. One of Herald's men ran to him with the reply from the ships. Falcon, Reed and Herald cheered as the ships turned and sailed toward the harbor.

A second boulder flew from *Tempest* striking the middle of the tower. It collapsed in a storm of stone.

"One more thing," laughed Falcon. "Please tell Ram that target practice is over".

ೞ   ೞ   ೞ   ೞ   ೞ

"We can't stay here forever," said Cilantra.

"We haven't been here half-a-day," replied Brock, a little defensively.

"It's a very nice cave," said Brittany, sweetly.

A light beam coming from above her made Brittany's hair glow like gold. Suddenly, the light flickered and went dark for a moment.

Brock raised his hand and hissed, "Quiet!"

"What is it?" whispered Cilantra.

"Someone's out there," said Brock nodding at the ceiling of the cave.

"The sunlight comes through holes in the rock. Somebody just blocked one."

"Maybe it was an animal," suggested Brittany.

Brock shook his head.

"Animals are smart enough to avoid the holes," he whispered. "Somebody's out there."

Two men knelt in the brush of the hilltop that formed the cave's roof. They lowered their heads close to a hole in the plateau and listened. The cave went silent. Smiling at one another they stood. Without a word the men ran down the hill.

ɞ   ɞ   ɞ   ɞ   ɞ

"Please stay here," pleaded Halston.

He stood with Quasar and Nemo on the palace portico. The six other Reds were already searching the palace.

"We can search too," said Nemo.

Halston shook his head.

"Brittany is my wife," said Quasar.

"I know," replied Halston. "And Falcon put you in charge. But we don't know what we'll find. Falcon will be displeased with me if you are hurt."

"We can take care of ourselves," said Quasar, hotly.

Halston shook his head and said simply, "You are unarmed," ending the discussion.

"Please stay here," he repeated.

"Fine," agreed Nemo, begrudgingly.

Halston looked Quasar in the eyes.

"And you?" he asked.

They stared at one another in silence until Quasar blinked.

"Fine," he said reluctantly.

Quasar and Nemo watched Halston as he ran into the palace and disappeared. They then moved to a stone bench near the edge of the portico and sat, dejectedly.

"Now what'll do we do?" asked Quasar, impatiently.

"We wait," replied Nemo.

A sudden sound from behind them caused Quasar and Nemo to jump from the bench.

Turning toward the garden, they were surprised to see a little girl standing peacefully with her hands at her side. The hem of her dress was torn and she was missing a shoe.

"Who are you?" asked Nemo.

"I'm Lee'a," she answered politely. "Who are you?"

"I'm Nemo," he answered, "and this is Quasar."

What is a little girl doing here all by herself, he thought?

"Oh, you're Quasar," said Lee'a with a smile. "Brittany will be glad you're here."

ೞ   ೞ   ೞ   ೞ   ೞ

King Ahala'nn stood alone looking down from the Upper Courtyard to the desert below. His personal guard formed a large half-circle around him. Their shields formed a protective wall.

Men and woman ran madly throughout the palace-fortress, all trying to prepare for the defense of Saalespor.

The king heard nothing and saw nothing but the massive buildup of forces outside the gates of his palace-fortress-prison.

"Your Majesty," cried General Ryguy Roces as he ran to the King.

The wall of shields opened to allow him passage to the King.

"If we can just hold out until the Navy comes," murmured the King. "We have food and water for many days. Our walls are thick, our towers tall."

The King smiled as a plan of defense formed in his mind.

"The desert sun is our friend," said the King. "They will roast before we fall."

"No, Your Majesty," said the general, simply. It was the first time he had ever said 'no' to the King.

"What?" said the king. He looked at the general in surprise.

"I have not known you to be a coward," said the King, harshly.

General Ryguy Roces stood his tallest allowing the words to strike him and recede like a wave upon a rock.

"Were I a coward," replied the general in measured tones, "I would have agreed with you."

General Ryguy Roces looked out at the main road. Troops in red, silver, yellow and green were massing along the road and spilling out into the nearby desert.

"The truth is, Your Majesty, we cannot hold out and we cannot win."

The general pointed in the distance.

"Can you see them?" he asked the King.

"I see strange towers swaying like trees in the desert wind," answered the King.

"There is no wind, Your Majesty," said the general. "The towers are moving up the main road, pulled by horses and men. They are coming."

"What of it?" asked the King.

"Those towers are machines of war, Your Majesty," said the general. "They will crash through the gates, break down the thick walls. Our high towers will crumble before them."

"How do you know these tales are true?" asked the King. "They sound like stories told by frightened old women."

Foolish pride and honest wisdom dueled in the King's heart.

"They are the last words I heard from my brother," said the general. "He saw them in the harbor and came to warn you."

The King heard a change in the general's voice. Surprisingly, he was wise enough to listen.

"Why have they come? What do they want?" shouted the King in frustration.

"I don't know," said General Ryguy Roces. "Why don't you ask them?"

The King did not seem to hear General Ryguy Roces. His eyes filled with tears as he mumbled, "What have you done? Oh Rhala'nn, what have you done?"

Suddenly, King Ahala'nn straightened his back and looked at General Ryguy Roces with passion in his eyes.

"Why don't you ask them, for me?"

ა ა ა ა ა

Quasar rode madly down the alley and through the iron gates. Nemo followed right behind him, with a little girl on the back of his horse. Lee'a squealed with delight as she was bumped and jostled by the ride. She wrapped her little arms tightly around Nemo's waste and held on with amazing strength.

Behind them rode the column of lancers and their saddle-mate Reds.

As he turned onto the main road, Quasar all but ran into one of Ram's massive war machines. The road was packed.

Quasar, Nemo and the column were all forced to slow down by the sheer number of troops on the road.

"Where is Lord Falcon?" shouted Quasar.

"He's at the front," shouted one man, uselessly. Quasar didn't know where the front was.

Another man pointed silently up the road.

A third said, "There's a palace-fortress at the top of the main road. Follow the road, you'll find him there."

"Thank you," shouted Quasar.

He began to kick his horse into a run when he realized there was nowhere for him to go. The road was jammed with soldiers, horses, carts, and huge rolling towers, all moving with the speed of a desert tortoise.

"I know another way," came a little voice.

Quasar looked over his shoulder to Nemo. "What?" he asked.

"To the palace," said Lee'a. "I know another way to the palace. This road's full."

"Are you sure?" asked Quasar.

"Yes I'm sure," she answered with a puzzled expression. "Can't you see the road is full?"

"Is he blind?" Lee'a whispered to Nemo. "My father's blind."

"No," laughed Nemo. "Can you really take us another way?"

"Sure," said Lee'a lightly. "My father told me lots of stories about the city and the desert and the King's palace."

Nemo looked deeply into her innocent eyes, but said nothing.

"Turn around," said Lee'a. "Just past the iron gate is a little round fountain with the dribble angel," she explained. "Turn there."

"The fountain!" cried Nemo in alarm. "We've forgotten Gibson at the fountain."

"Follow me," shouted Nemo.

Without waiting for Quasar to say anything, Nemo turned his horse and headed down the road. Immediately past the iron gate they found the little round fountain, and two columns of lancers, impatiently waiting.

"There you are," shouted Gibson. "We were about to come find you."

"We have important news for Falcon," cried Quasar.

"And we were wanted at the front an hour ago," replied Gibson, angrily.

"I can get us to the palace," said Lee'a, sweetly. "My father told me about it all the time. He's blind but he knows everything."

"Who is this?" asked Gibson between clenched teeth.

"I'm Lee'a," she answered politely. "Who are you?"

"This is Gibson," answered Nemo. "He's really a nice man when he's not grumpy," said Nemo. He gave a cautionary glance at Gibson.

"Pleased to meet you," said Gibson in a flat voice.

"Can she really get us to the front?" asked Gibson.

"The front of what?" asked Lee'a.

"The front of the King's palace," answered Nemo.

"Sure," answered Lee'a innocently. "Go that way," she said pointing with her little fingers. "Ride fast again," she said happily. "I'll tell you when to turn."

She wrapped her little arms around Nemo and cried, "Ride fast again!"

Quasar, Gibson, Halston six Reds and twenty-one lancers thundered off behind Nemo. He led them through a secluded neighborhood of large, deserted houses. They passed a dozen abandoned houses, all surrounded by lush gardens and enclosed by walls.

"Turn left at the tree," laughed Lee'a.

She laughed because her voice sounded all bouncy and funny from riding so quickly.

The lane emptied onto a hilly desert trail.

"Just keep going," cried Lee'a. "You'll see. My father told me stories."

Gibson shouted something and waved his hand. The three columns merged into one.

They rode higher and higher into the hilly desert. On their right the trail was dotted with green shrubs and lush trees.

"Keep to your left," cried Lee'a.

When he reached the anticipated fork in the road, Nemo veered left. The long column followed quickly behind him immersed in a sandy cloud of dust.

☙ ☙ ☙ ☙ ☙

High in the hilly desert, Cilantra led her horse out from the cave into daylight; behind her came Brittany, followed by Brock and his horse.

She stopped, waiting for her eyes to adjust to the bright desert sun.

Squinting into the distance, Cilantra noticed a long dust cloud winding its way along a trail.

"What do you make of that?" she asked, pointing.

Brock and Brittany joined Cilantra. They did not hear the two men who crept nearer and nearer from above. The men were armed with knives and rods. Below, five others armed with knives and nets, closed the snare.

☙ ☙ ☙ ☙ ☙

Falcon, Reed, Shank and Herald were at the great round table in the Command Tent when Ram burst in. He was hot, sweaty, exhausted and couldn't be happier.

"Six," bellowed Ram, bursting past the two members of the Service of Light who guarded the tent entrance.

"I'll have six standing before the walls, armed and ready, in less than an hour!"

"Ram," cried Falcon. "It's good to see you. Come in and cool off."

"I don't have time," cried Ram.

"Well, let's make time," insisted Falcon. "We have much to discuss and much to tell you," he said.

"Like what?" asked Ram, somewhat surprised.

"Like where we want to put your machines and how we want to use them."

Ram stood without speaking for a long time. His face was frozen in a frown.

Falcon, Reed, Shank and Herald looked at one another. They could not mask their concern for Ram.

Within the Command Tent were hung large silk sheets in the colors of the House of

Hiram; Red for Falcon, Green for Reed, Yellow for Shank, Purple for Ram, etc. The back part of the tent was hung with the great veil of shields.

"You look thirsty, brother," said Shank, handing Ram a large mug of water. "Come, sit at the table," he said lightly.

Shank pulled out the chair that was in front of Ram's purple banner. He motioned for his brother to sit.

Ram took the mug but did not drink and did not sit.

"We have so much to tell you," said Herald. "Perhaps, Gannon should start."

"Gannon?" asked Ram. "I thought he was aboard *Scorpion.*"

"I was," said a voice from behind the veil of shields. "Now I'm here."

Gannon walked through the veil to the table and hugged Ram. He moved with a confidence he had not previously known.

"It's good to see you Ram," said Gannon.

"And you, little brother," replied Ram.

Ram smiled and tried to shake the confusion from his mind.

"I, too, am here," said a deep familiar voice from behind the veil.

"Father," exclaimed Ram!

His confusion increased.

Ram wiped the sweat from his face and tried to smooth his dirty, wrinkled uniform with his dirty, sweaty hands.

"I didn't know," stammered Ram. "I thought you were aboard *Vengeance.*

"We were," said the Lord Hiram stepping from behind the veil.

"Gannon and I landed a short while ago and came up from the beach," explained the Lord Hiram.

"We have much to tell you," he said. "We have much to tell everyone. All your brothers will soon be here and we will talk."

"Of course, Father," said Ram.

He raised the mug to his lips and drained it in one long drink.

Light streamed into the tent as a guard opened the tent flap.

"Lord Reed, a word with you, sir," began the man, but stopped short when he saw the Lord Hiram.

"I'm sorry to interrupt, sir," said the man. His face was as green as his uniform.

"Enter," said the Lord Hiram, not unkindly.

When the man hesitated, Reed added, "Really, you're fine, please come in."

The man stepped within the Command Tent and tried to deliver his message. He first looked at Lord Reed, to whom the message had been sent, but then he looked to Lord Falcon the eldest brother and Commander. Finally, the man turned and faced the Lord Hiram.

"King Ahala'nn of Saalespor has sent a message," began the Green. "He wishes to send an emissary...," he continued.

Taking out a parchment the Green read; *...an emissary to discuss the cessation of hostilities and avoid needless bloodshed on both sides.*

"So says the King's message," concluded the man.

"He wishes to keep his kingdom and his head," said the Lord Hiram with a smile. "This I can understand."

"Falcon," asked the Lord Hiram, "what say you?"

"I will meet with this emissary, but he must be a man of some import, able to speak in the name of King Ahala'nn."

Falcon signaled to Reed with a slight nod of his head.

"Arrange the meeting," ordered Reed.

"Yes sir," replied the Green.

The Green stepped from the tent. Once outside, he took a deep, deep breath.

Two members of the Service of Light stood on either side of the tent entrance. One closed the tent flap without speaking.

The man glanced at them.

I only expected to speak with Lord Reed, thought the man. *Why didn't anyone tell me who was in there.*

As the man ran from the tent, Lords Tulmar, Norrom and Vine arrived on horseback. One of the guards opened the tent flap for them. They went straight into the Command Tent.

The House of Hiram met for their final counsel of war for before battle. They reminded themselves of their goals, strengths and weaknesses. Falcon paced around the table while he spoke.

"First and foremost," declared Falcon, "we must find my wife and Brittany. If they live, we must rescue them above all else."

"And if they don't live," asked Tulmar?

The table erupted at the question.

"Of course they live," shouted Norrom.

"How can you ask that?" cried Vine.

"Forgive me," said Tulmar, loudly, "but I too am married. I know what I would want to do if someone kidnapped my Blanche, much less killed her."

As he spoke, Tulmar slammed his massive fist on the table.

Tulmar was second born and stood half a head taller than Falcon. His arms had grown to the size of small trees, fed by years at the forge and anvil. He looked like a young twin of the Lord Hiram.

Falcon stood perfectly still with his head bowed. Until this moment he had never thought it possible that Cilantra could really be killed.

Tulmar looked up from the table and realized he had pained his older brother.

"Forgive me, Falcon" said Tulmar, quietly. "I have stupidly added to your burden."

Tulmar rose and walked to where his brother stood. He embraced Falcon in his massive arms.

"It was an honest question," admitted Falcon. "But one I hope we never need answer." Falcon paused before continuing.

"Let us discuss it only if the time comes when we need to discuss it," said Falcon.

Everyone nodded their agreement.

"But if that time comes, Tulmar," said Falcon with a voice of steal. "I will hear what you would want to do and add some thoughts of my own."

A hush came upon the tent as his brothers and father saw Falcon as they had never see him before. His eyes, his face revealed how very fearsome Falcon could be.

"This evil came upon Cilantra and Brittany for no reason," said Falcon. "They did nothing to warrant it. We must commit to getting them back, safe and whole. This is first. We right the wrong and then we deal with the wrong-doers."

Falcon came to stand at his place at the table.

"What say you?" he asked.

As he had seen his father do, Falcon looked intently at each man around the table. Each answered him in turn. They met his gaze with clear eyes and full understanding. They all agreed.

The rest of the meeting was merely details. When all was discussed and argued and planned and everyone had said what they needed to say, the Lord Hiram stood.

"There is one more thing Gannon and I need to explain you," began the Lord Hiram.

He nodded to his youngest son and sat down. Gannon stood and smiled shyly as he looked around the table.

"You all know," said Gannon, "that *Vengeance and Scorpion* have kept away from the fleet."

The brothers all nodded their heads and listened politely.

"Some of you may have heard that *Scorpion* carries a very special passenger," said Gannon.

"It's a girl," said Vine with a wink. "Have you found a girl, a wife, little brother?" he asked.

Gannon blushed. "No, it's not about a girl," he said. To make matters worse, his voice cracked.

"He's getting married," said Norrom. "Are you getting married, Gannon?" asked Norrom in mock seriousness.

"No I'm not," cried Gannon. "*Scorpion* has a very special passenger."

"He can't get married before me," cried Vine, ignoring Gannon. "I'm older. In fact, Reed and I are both older. We get married first."

"I'm older than all three of you," said Ram, "so I get married first."

"I'm sorry Ram," said Norrom, "but nobody's wants to marry you. You don't bathe enough. Besides, I'm older than all four of you."

The Lord Hiram stood. Except for a few snorts and giggles, the tent quickly quieted down.

"I bathe enough," mumbled Ram.

"What Gannon has to say is important," began the Lord Hiram, "but first I have something to say."

"I want you to be assured," said the Lord Hiram, "that I will find wives for all of you who are not married."

The married sons, Falcon, Tulmar and Shank, erupted in hysterics.

The unmarried ones, Herald, Norrom, Ram, Vine and Reed, sat with their mouths wide open.

"I will make sure," continued the Lord Hiram with a smile, "to find you all big, healthy Porco wives!"

For a counsel of war, there was an awful lot of laughing. But sometimes, even in the gravest situation, people need to laugh.

When they got control of themselves, Gannon stood and said, "We have brought a very special passenger who will help us win."

"At hearing this, the House of Hiram became deadly serious.

Please, Gannon," said Falcon. "Tell us about this very secret and very special passenger."

Suddenly, the tent flap opened and bright sunlight streamed in, blinding everyone for a moment.

The flap closed, the light receded and there stood Quasar, Nemo and a little girl.

"Forgive us Lord Hiram," said Quasar, formally; "but we have news that cannot wait."

"Speak," commanded the Lord Hiram.

Quasar stepped to Falcon and put his hand on Falcon's shoulder.

"They're alive," said Quasar with a great smile. "Cilantra and Brittany are alive!"

He showed Falcon a thin white ribbon decorated by tiny embroidered flowers.

"They're alive," he repeated.

The tent erupted in a chorus of joyful questions.

"Are you sure?" asked Tulmar.

"How do you know?" added Herald.

"Great news!" shouted Ram.

"Where are they?" asked Reed.

"This is Lee'a," replied Nemo.

He raised his hand, signaling for quiet.

"She served Cilantra and Brittany until this morning, when they escaped," he said as he gently pushed the little girl forward.

The tent became silent.

"Lee'a has a lot to tell us," said Quasar. "Hear her."

In her own way, Lee'a told them of Prince Rhala'nn and his Spotters, Takers and Favored Ones.

As he listened, Falcon's anger turned into a kind of rage that he had never before known. He became more and more controlled and quiet, yet more and more determined.

Lee'a told of how Cilantra and Brittany had arranged for them to get out of the palace and of the walk on the beach, and of *Emeraldsea*.

She described coming for the breakfast trays that very morning and finding the red silk rope dangling from the terrace and the dead guards at the bottom of the rope.

Her story was cut short by a blaze of light as the tent flap was again opened.

It was the same Green who had entered the Command Tent before.

"Forgive me my Lords," said the man.

He sounded more confident than the last time, but seeing the little girl and Quasar and Nemo confused him all the more.

"The Lord Falcon is needed," he said simply.

"What is it?" ask Falcon.

"The gates are opening, sir. The emissary is coming."

ᘓ   ᘓ   ᘓ   ᘓ   ᘓ

King Ahala'nn looked down from the Upper Courtyard. Below, he could see the steep lane that ran from the gates to the road. He could also see the colorful forces of the House of Hiram spread out in every direction.

Six massive towers had been rolled up in the last hour and now faced the palace-fortress.

"What surprises do you bring?" said the King to the towers. "I'm sure I'll hear from you soon enough."

The King was feeling totally alone and for good reason. Having ordered his personal guard to go with General Ryguy Roces, he was indeed totally alone.

"I'm afraid you will have much greater need of them than I, General," said the King upon giving the order.

The King would not hear any of the general's thoughts to the contrary.

Below, the Common Courtyard was filled with soldiers performing tasks of every description. They all stopped what they were doing as General Ryguy Roces and the King's guard moved through the courtyard.

The general sat upon a white horse in his finest uniform. In his gloved right hand he held his sword by the blade; from its hilt hung a white flag of truce. The King's personal guard stood around him.

"Open!" cried General Ryguy Roces.

Six sentries gave a mighty cry as they lifted the wooden beam that secured the gates. Then three men grabbed the right side of the doors and three grabbed the left. With a mighty effort, the men opened the huge main gates.

Instantly, the King's guard rushed through the opening and formed a protective wall of shields.

King Ahala'nn smiled when he saw the precision and bravery of his personal guard.

General Ryguy Roces nudged his horse forward. Slowly, the general and the guard made their way down the steep lane toward the main road.

A formation of twelve men walked along the main road to the bottom of the steep lane. They wore the sky blue uniform of Lord Herald.

Raising golden trumpets to their lips the men blew a long regal flurry. It rebounded off the fortress walls and echoed through the desert hills.

General Ryguy Roces motioned to his guards. "You may go no further," he said. "Thank you for your service."

The guards stopped and lowered their shields.

General Ryguy Roces continued riding down the lane toward the main road. He was totally exposed to any archer's arrow.

A lone horseman rode up the steep lane to meet him.

That is the strongest man and the biggest horse I have ever seen, thought the general. *I hope they're not all like that.*

"I am Lord Tulmar, second born of the House of Hiram," announced the horseman.

General Ryguy Roces extended his arm and handed his sword to Lord Tulmar.

"You may keep your sword, General," said Tulmar in response. "Follow me, please."

Tulmar turned and led the general onto the main road. An honor guard of one hundred Silver Lancers lined the road. Tulmar and the general rode without speaking until they came to the Command Tent.

The tent was flanked on both sides by Reds, Greens and Yellows. High, at the top of the tent flew the Twin Black Hawks on a field of gold. Two members of the Service of Light stood on either side of the tent entrance.

A Silver took the reins of the general's horse in hand, without speaking.

"General," said Tulmar in a deep thunderous voice. "Lord Falcon, first born of the House of Hiram will see you now."

"Thank you," said General Ryguy Roces, as he dismounted.

The Silver led the general's horse away, leaving him standing before the Command Tent.

Members of the Service of Light on both sides of the entrance lifted the tent flaps; light flooded in. There stood Lord Falcon, dressed in blood red; around his waist hung the huge double-edged broadsword of the House of Hiram. In his left hand he held the mighty Golden Rod.

"Welcome General," said Falcon. "Please come in."

He turned and walked to his place at the great round table. General Ryguy Roces entered the tent and the guards closed the flaps.

ൠ   ൠ   ൠ   ൠ   ൠ

High in the Upper Courtyard, King Ahala'nn scanned the horizon.

"Oh, Rhala'nn ," said the King aloud. "If only the Navy would return. We could drive these intruders from the precious sands of Saalespor."

The King smiled at the thought.

"They would never expect an attack from the sea."

As he thought and dreamed, a flash of light in the distance caught his attention.

"What was that? Could it be," the King mused?

The King strained to see more.

A Green, hidden at the edge of the desert, also saw the flash of light. The hair on the back of his neck stood up. Waiting, watching, all of his senses became heightened.

There it is, again, thought the Green.

Abandoning stealth and secrecy, the Green ran with all his strength toward the encampment.

Within the Command Tent, Lord Falcon fixed his steely eyes on General Ryguy Roces.

"How could he not know?" cried Falcon. "He is your king!"

Falcon called upon all his self-control to remain calm.

"You say the Prince kidnapped women, raided lands, sold slaves, and the King knew nothing of it?"

Hidden behind the veil of shields, the Lord Hiram squeezed the arms of his chair so hard that his knuckles turned white.

That man is lucky Falcon doesn't kill him where he sits, thought the Lord Hiram.

General Ryguy Roces took a deep breath before answering.

"The King has been overly lenient with his son," admitted the general.

"General," said Falcon in greatly measured tones. "One of the women he kidnapped was my wife!"

All color drained from the general's face, but he sat resolute. A lessor man might have run from the tent, so fierce was Falcon's countenance.

"Lord Falcon," said the general, in as tranquil a voice as he could manage. "I see now why you have come."

General Ryguy Roces stood slowly.

"King Ahala'nn will be deeply grieved to learn of this," said the general, slowly. "In his name, first, let me apologize and beg your forgiveness," he continued humbly.

"The King knew nothing of this, I can assure you. I doubt the Prince knew who your wife was," he added as an afterthought.

The general bowed his head to Falcon and then again took his seat at the table.

Lord Falcon sat back in his chair and scrutinized the face of this young general.

If he is lying, thought Falcon, *I cannot see it.*

"It will not be as easy as that, General," said Falcon, finally.

He struggled to not avenge his wife here and now, but his own words in the counsel of war proved to be his strength.

First and foremost, remembered Falcon, *we must find my wife and Brittany and rescue them above all else.*

"First and foremost," declared Falcon, "You must return Lady Cilantra and her friend, Brittany, immediately."

General Ryguy Roces nodded his head in agreement.

"We will decide more after we learn how they have been treated," said Falcon.

"Second," continued Falcon, "the other so called 'Favored Ones', will be freed."

How does he know about them, thought the general? He again nodded his head in agreement.

"Third," said Falcon, with great control. "Prince Rhala'nn will be given to us for immediate justice."

The mind of General Ryguy Roces raced to find a way to answer. He knew his life and the future of Saalespor rested on what he now said.

"Thank you Lord Falcon," began the general. "This grave wrong shall be righted," he declared.

"We will gladly return Lady Cilantra, her friend Brittany and the other Favored Ones, as soon as they can be found."

The general looked at Falcon whose eyes narrowed at the words *as soon as they can be found*.

"As for the Prince," continued the general carefully, "I am afraid we cannot give him to you."

Falcon rose slowly, menacingly from his seat. The general kept his, and raised an open palmed hand toward him.

"Hear me, Lord Falcon," said the general quickly. "Please."

Self-control is like a muscle. When well exercised, it can be strong when needed. Falcon used all his strength to sit and listen.

"I am sure the King would give his son to you for justice," explained the general, "but justice has been brought upon the Prince, already."

"What do you mean," asked Falcon?

"Lord Falcon," said the general. "Prince Rhala'nn is dead."

Falcon breathed in deeply. His nostrils flared like those of a warhorse.

"How can this be?" asked Falcon. "Speak truth, General," warned Falcon. "One lie and all of Saalespor will burn."

"I do not lie," said the general, temper rising in his voice.

This was the most dangerous time of the meeting. The tension grew between these two men. Veins in Falcon's neck began to throb. The huge muscles in the general's arms twitched. Behind the veil of shields, the Lord Hiram stood, ready to intervene.

General Ryguy Roces lowered his voice and continued.

"The Prince was killed this very day," said General Ryguy Roces.

"How?" asked Falcon. He did not believe the general.

The general remembered the events of the morning. He relived the arrival in the Upper Courtyard of his brother Hacim, bloodied and dying. In his mind's eye he saw again the body of Prince Rhala'nn and his blood on the courtyard.

"Some say he was killed by one of the King's personal guard," answered the general. He paused, and then added quietly, "But this is not true."

General Ryguy Roces looked down at the table before continuing. Strangely, he noticed the beautiful shield of pure gold inlaid at the center of the table. It was etched with the image of twin black hawks.

The general looked Falcon in the eyes. "The King killed his own son," said the general.

No words had ever been harder for him to speak.

Stunned, the Lord Hiram sat down behind the veil of shields. A look of disbelief filled Falcon's face.

"Lord Falcon," said the general, quietly. "The sins Prince Rhala'nn committed against you are grave. But believe me, graver still are the sins he committed against his father and mother."

Silence hung in the tent like a dense fog. Falcon did not know what to say. For a son to sin against his father; for a father to kill his son, this was beyond anything Falcon could imagine.

There was a stirring in the tent; a slight sound of metal against metal. Falcon and the general turned absentmindedly toward the sound.

There, before the veil of shields, stood the Lord Hiram, a good father and righteous king.

Falcon jumped to his feet and stood at attention. The general did likewise.

"General," Falcon said formally. "May I present my father, the Lord Hiram. Father, this is General Ryguy Roces."

"Please sit," said the Lord Hiram. Without waiting, he continued.

"We have heard many words. Now is the time for your King to act," proclaimed the Lord Hiram.

"There is time before the sunsets, General," said Hiram. "Lady Cilantra and Brittany will be safe within my camp this day, or destruction will rain upon Saalespor the likes of which you cannot imagine."

The Lord Hiram's voice was calm and quiet, yet fear penetrated General Ryguy Roces to his very heart.

"Tribute for spending our blood and treasure will come later," said Hiram. "One thing more," said the Lord Hiram. "We must see the body of this prince, today!"

"I will do all that I can," promised General Ryguy Roces.

"Do not fail in this, General," warned the Lord Hiram.

Without another word, he clapped his hands. Members of the Service of Light opened the tent flap and rushed in. Seeing that all was well, they escorted the general from the tent.

"He is an honorable man," declared Hiram. "I hope his king is also."

Falcon nodded and watched the general through the opening in the tent.

"In another time and place," said Falcon, "I think we could have been friends."

The general mounted his horse and rode swiftly to his king.

CHAPTER 9
A Very Special Passenger

$\mathcal{T}$he King looked at General Ryguy Roces as if he were mad.

"No," he shouted again. "I will not give them the body of my precious son."

"Your precious son?" asked the general.

The King glared at his loyal general.

"Do not forget yourself, General," hissed the King.

"Your Majesty forgets," said the general. "It is the actions of your treacherous son that has brought your kingdom into peril."

"How dare you!" shouted the King.

"Your Majesty," said the general. "Everyone knows."

The King narrowed his eyes and glared at his loyal general.

"Knows what?" asked the King.

"Your son poisoned the Queen; your wife, his mother," replied the general.

The King wanted to rage against General Ryguy Roces, but the truth of it all could no longer be hidden.

"Three times we protected you from his poison," said the general.

The King looked blankly at General Ryguy Roces.

"This army is here because he kidnapped their wives," shouted the general.

The King did not respond.

"Let your son stop in death what he started in life. Give them the proof they need."

The King's face was as if it were carved in stone. He neither moved nor spoke.

"Your Majesty," said the general, calming himself. "I have met with these people. They are honorable. Show them what you have done and thus save your kingdom."

"What I have done?" barked the King. "Prince Rhala'nn was killed by one of your men!"

"No, Your Majesty," said the general, sadly. "I would gladly claim the credit, but it was not one of my men."

The King turned and looked out toward the forces of the House of Hiram that were arrayed against him. It was a strangely beautiful sight.

"You have said, Your Majesty," began the general, quietly, "that you still have time to right many wrongs."

General Ryguy Roces spoke to the King as a loving son to his father.

"Your time runs out at sundown. Do what they ask and right the wrong."

The King looked long at the general. "If only you had been my son," he said. "I tell you the truth, Ryguy," said the King. "I knew little about the Favored Ones then, and I know nothing about where they are, now. I cannot give them their wives," said the King.

"Then at least give them proof that justice was served," replied the general. "Give them the body of Prince Rhala'nn."

ೞ   ೞ   ೞ   ೞ   ೞ

"Where is the Lord Falcon?" shouted the Green excitedly.

He ran past the sentry, a young Green, without even stopping for an answer.

"He's in the Command Tent," cried the sentry, but the man was gone.

The man continued running as if chased by dragons. As he entered the edge of the compound he spied another Green sentry.

"Where is the Lord Falcon?" the man shouted.

"He's in the Command Tent," answered the sentry.

The man stopped to catch his breath. Embarrassed, he forced himself to ask, "Where is the Command Tent?

"Didn't you see the general come from the fortress?" asked the sentry.

"What?" asked the man.

"Lord Falcon and the Porco general are meeting in the Command Ten, right now," replied the man.

"Where is Lord Reed, then?' asked the man.

The sentry shrugged his shoulders. "What's so important?" he asked.

"What about Lord Quasar the Dragon-Slayer?" asked the man.

Clearly, the man had urgent news.

"Lords Quasar and Nemo rode in with a column of Silvers and Reds a short while ago," replied the sentry.

He pointed to a section of the camp where horses were kept.

"They are probably over there," he said. "They had a little girl with them," added the sentry, but the man was already running toward the horses.

⅌   ⅌   ⅌   ⅌   ⅌

The Lord Hiram and his nine living sons sat around the table in the Command Tent. Lord Falcon and his father recounted their impressions of General Ryguy Roces and the conditions that had been discussed with him.

The conversation now revolved around Ram and the use of his machines of war.

"No!" said Ram for the third time. "We should NOT wait until sundown. We should let the bombardment begin now, while they can still see their destruction."

Ram stood from the table and roamed angrily and aimlessly inside the tent. He even knocked over the great Golden Rod as it stood in its holder. Fortunately, he caught it.

"Sorry," he said looking sheepishly at his family. He smiled in embarrassment. It reminded his father of Ram when he was a little boy.

The Lord Hiram stood and walked to his seventh son. Ram, he knew, needed to prove himself as useful in battle as his six older brothers; especially after being of such little use at Draamor.

Falcon, Shank and Kyler had all seen battle; Kyler being killed at Three Rivers. As for Tulmar, though not actually in battle himself, his work in weapons and metallurgy had shown his value time and time again.

Herald and his men were constantly being called upon to signal troops and ships while Norrom, as admiral of the Navy, was involved in everything the House of Hiram did.

Though all his sons loved and respected one another, the Lord Hiram knew that Ram needed to prove himself, to himself as well as to his brothers.

Ram's younger brother, Vine, didn't seem to care about being in actual battle. He always said he was too busy feeding everyone.

An army that's hungry is an army that loses,
Vine was fond of saying.

Reed had proven especially gifted in warning the family of peril through his vast network of spies and informants.

Now, even Gannon, the youngest, had been entrusted with a very special passenger.

The Lord Hiram put his arm around his Ram's shoulder.

"I understand, son," said the Lord Hiram, quietly. "We all know how important your machines are," he said.

All of Ram's brothers nodded in agreement.

"They are impressive," said Falcon.

"You killed the dragons at Draamor," said Norrom.

"That was only luck," replied Ram, gloomily. "And those shots came from *Eclipse*, one of your ships," he said to Norrom. "Most of my machines ended up at the bottom of the sea."

"Brother," said the Lord Falcon. "We cannot start the bombardment now. I have given them until sundown to return Cilantra and Brittany and prove their prince is dead."

Falcon looked hard at his brother.

"Would you have me risk their lives and break my word so that you can show the power of your machines?"

Ram looked at Falcon and blinked. It was difficult for him to think when he was so angry. Ram drew in several deep breaths, sounding not unlike a big bear. As his temper cooled his mind sharpened.

"No," replied Ram as he returned to his seat at the table. "It can wait."

Without warning, the tent flap flew open and a man rushed in. Guards from the Service of Light rushed in with him. Bright sunlight blinded everyone in the tent.

Falcon drew his sword and stood between his father and the intruder. His brothers jumped from the table, drawing their weapons.

"Falcon, Falcon," cried the voice of Quasar. His eyes were red from weeping.

"I almost killed you," shouted Falcon, as he put back his sword. He then noticed that his own right arm was in his father's restraining grip.

"No fear of that," smiled the Lord Hiram.

The others again took their places at the table, all murmuring.

"I'm sorry Falcon," said Quasar, "but it couldn't wait."

Fear gripped Falcon's heart as he noticed Quasar's red eyes.

"What is it?" asked Falcon.

Just then, the Service of Light stepped aside and through the radiant daylight walked Cilantra.

Falcon froze at the heavenly sight. She seemed encased in white light, like a vision, like an angel.

"Cilantra," gasped Falcon.

He rushed to her and wrapped her in his arms. She melted into his embrace.

Behind her came Brittany and Brock.

Quasar quickly moved to her side and put his arm around her. They already had their first moment of reunion, but Quasar just couldn't stop looking at her and holding her in his arms.

There was much crying, hugging, kissing and tender words; all too private to write here.

Finally, the Lord Hiram closed his eyes and lifting an arm straight up, as was his custom, offered a prayer of thanks.

"Who knows of this?" asked Hiram.

Cilantra wiped the tears from her face and answered, "Only the Greens who found us and the Service of Light who brought us in here."

Reed grinned uncontrollably when he heard it was his men who found them. Ram scowled jealously for a moment, but then broke into a huge smile, himself.

"Good job, brother," said Ram.

"This must remain a secret for now," said Hiram. "We will have to see what King Ahala'nn says. It will tell us if he can be trusted."

Smiling at Cilantra, the Lord Hiram, said, "I must ask you and Brittany to remain in this tent for a little while."

"Of course," replied Cilantra. Brittany nodded her head.

"Falcon, Quasar," said Hiram in mock sternness, "I order you to remain here, too!"

His face blossomed into a huge grin and he laughed aloud at his own joke.

"The rest of my sons," said the Lord Hiram, "should go find something else to do."

The brothers stood, laughing and began making their way out of the tent.

"Brock!" said the Lord Hiram.

He was surprised to see the man standing by the tent flap.

"Hello, sir," said Brock. He was not sure what he should say or do.

"You look hungry," said the Lord Hiram.

"No, I'm fine, thank you," replied Brock, honestly.

The Lord Hiram frowned a little and smiled at the same time.

"You look hungry," he said again.

"Vine," ordered the Lord Hiram. "Take Brock here to your food tent and get him something to eat and drink."

"Yes, sir," replied Vine.

"This way Brock," said Vine gesturing toward the tent flap.

"Right," said Brock, blushing.

He glanced at Falcon, Cilantra, Quasar and Brittany.

"Right, I'm very hungry, now that you mention it."

He followed Vine out of the tent.

The rest of the House of Hiram exited the tent, leaving Falcon and Quasar a moment of solitude and sweet reunion with their wives.

The Lord Hiram put his arm around Ram and said, "Son, would you please show your machines to me?"

ᆼᎢ   ᆼᎢ   ᆼᎢ   ᆼᎢ   ᆼᎢ

From his perch on the Upper Courtyard King Ahala'nn looked at the horizon.

"The sun will set soon enough, yet still they do nothing," said the King. "They are toothless dogs barking at shadows."

"They are honorable men, Your Majesty," replied General Ryguy Roces. "They gave us until sundown which is why they haven't attacked. Let us be honorable also, and do what they ask."

"We don't know where their women are," replied the King. We have most of the others, but their wives have vanished."

"Then tell them the truth," pleaded the general.

"Enough!" cried the King. "Are you my counselor or my general?" he asked sarcastically. "I am finished with this discussion."

As the King spoke, row upon row of archers marched through the Upper Courtyard and took up positions along the wall.

"What are you doing?" cried the general.

"If you don't know what I am doing," hissed the King, "you are not the general I thought you to be."

"Ready longbows," shouted the King.

 CB   CB   CB   CB   CB

As they walked among his towers, Ram blissfully explained the gears and levers that made the catapults work. The Lord Hiram had seen it all before, of course, but he wanted to affirm his son by seeing it all again. Hiram hoped the machines would not have to be used today, but that did not mean he didn't think them valuable.

"How quickly can they be armed and ready?" asked the Lord Hiram.

"I'm glad you asked," said Ram.

He ran to one of Herald's signalmen who had been assigned to him for just this purpose, and gave the order.

The man lifted a horn to his lips and blew a signal that was meant just for Ram's men. Special signalmen at each of the towers repeated the signal in response.

Around the towers Ram's Purples leaped into action.

Some began pulling mightily on the gear wheels that winched the catapult arm and bucket. Other's moved carts loaded with boulders closer to the machines.

Ram's men strained to load the catapults with boulders from the carts. At each tower a signalman waited to wave a purple flag as soon as the machine was armed and ready. The tower at which Ram and his father stood was first to be ready. Ram proudly watched as flags at the other towers were waved.

"All armed and ready, sir" said Ram turning to his father.

He was shocked to find the Lord Hiram down on one knee with an arrow sticking from his side. Two members of the ever-present Service of Light lay dead at his side.

"Father," cried Ram!

೮ʒ   ೮ʒ   ೮ʒ   ೮ʒ   ೮ʒ

The King smiled to see so many of the enemy fall in the first volley of arrows.

"No!" screamed General Ryguy Roces. "Stop, you must stop!"

"Light your arrows!" commanded the King.

All along the wall of the Upper Courtyard archers set the tips of their arrows aflame.

"No!" screamed General Ryguy Roces.

"Target the towers," shouted the King; "Ready longbows. Shoot!"

ଔ ଔ ଔ ଔ ଔ

A dozen members of the Service of Light surrounded the Lord Hiram, shielding him with their bodies.

"I'm fine," said Hiram, but there was a low gurgling sound in his voice as he spoke.

"You have an arrow sticking out of you, Father," said Ram. "You're not fine."

Ignoring his son, the Lord Hiram shouted to a nearby signalman.

"Tell Gannon it is time for these Porco to meet his special passenger."

With that, the Lord Hiram allowed the Service of White to carry him to safety.

Ram followed his father half-way to the healing tents when he glimpsed his towers.

"No! No!" he cried out.

He left his father in the care of the Service of Light and ran back toward the towers. All of them were aflame.

The machines were made of wood, but great strong beams, like those of a catapult, are hard to light on fire. The tower part, however, was actually made to act as a shield for the men working on the catapult. To save weight, they were made of woven reeds; lighter than wood but still strong enough to stop arrows.

The danger of fire was supposed to be alleviated by soaking the reeds with water before going into battle; something Ram had not yet ordered.

"Release, release" shouted Ram.

With a great mechanical noise the machines began launching their payloads at the palace-fortress. Unfortunately, the fire had already weakened the ropes that worked the catapults. Some snapped, whipping the ground around the towers with burning fiber.

The boulders flew into the air, but some fell short while others struck harmlessly at the thick base of the fortress wall.

Cʒ Cʒ Cʒ Cʒ Cʒ

The King laughed when he saw the success of his arrows and the failure of the catapults.

"You see, Ryguy," said King Ahala'nn, "this is how a king acts. We will hold them off until the Navy returns and then we will enslave them all. What a price they will bring."

"What did you say?" asked General Ryguy Roces.

A seed of a thought began to bloom for the general.

"You knew about the slave trade all along," said the general. "You knew about the kidnappings."

"Ready longbows," shouted the King; "Shoot!"

Another volley rained death upon the forces of the House of Hiram.

"Of course, I knew," sneered the King. "I knew about everything my ambitious little offspring was doing. He just didn't know I knew."

"Why?" asked the general, as his heart was breaking.

"Slave trade is a dangerous business," said the King. "I let Rhala'nn do all the work and take all the risk." The King smiled, wickedly.

"This last shipment was the biggest anyone has ever attempted. Rhala'nn would have been proud." The King laughed.

"I recently got word that all the merchandise has been sold and the Navy is on its way home with the gold," said the King.

He spoke as if he had sold a crop of silk worms.

"Rhala'nn probably heard the news too," said the King coldly, "so I had to adjust his plans."

"Now General," ordered the King, "do your job. Go to the Common Courtyard and make sure the main gate is secure. We still have a lot of work to do before the Navy arrives."

General Ryguy Roces ran from the Upper Courtyard, unsure of what he would do next.

೦೩   ೦೩   ೦೩   ೦೩   ೦೩

Falcon and Quasar stepped out of the Command Tent. They were surprised to find that the Service of Light no longer guarded the tent. Noise and confusion flew around them like flies around last week's fish.

Cilantra and Brittany peered through the opening of the tent.

"What has happened," asked Cilantra?

"I don't know," said Falcon.

"Look," cried Brittany, pointing into the sky; "The towers!"

"Stay here, please," said Falcon as he began to move toward the burning towers.

"You too, please," said Quasar to Brittany.

"What has happened," shouted Falcon to a Red who was running nearby?

"Lord Falcon," replied the man

He stopped running, realizing that Falcon had not yet heard the news.

"I am so sorry," he said, "but the Lord Hiram was felled by an arrow."

"What!" cried Falcon.

The news struck him like an arrow in his heart.

"They attacked without warning, without honor," said the man. "The Service of Light brought him to the healing tents."

"Thank you," mumbled Falcon. "Don't let me keep you."

Having been dismissed, the Red continued on his way.

"I want to go to the healing tents," said Cilantra. "We can see the Lord Hiram," she suggested. "Maybe we can help."

"And there must be other wounded," added Brittany. "We can help them, too."

"We can all go," said Falcon.

"You will be needed here, Falcon," said a strong voice from behind.

Falcon turned and looked into the face of his brother, Tulmar. Behind him were Shank, Herald, and Norrom. Their faces were pale and angry.

"We are under attack, Falcon," said Tulmar. "Let the healers do their job."

"And we shall do ours," added Shank.

"May we go?" asked Cilantra.

"Yes," replied Falcon. "Please send me word on Father," he asked.

"Please be careful," said Quasar as he hugged Brittany.

Letting their wives leave so soon after being reunited was one of the hardest things Falcon and Quasar ever had to do.

Vine and Brock came running up to the Command Tent. "How bad is he?" asked Vine.

"We don't know," replied Tulmar.

"It's not good," came Ram's deep, despondent voice. He ran up from behind Tulmar.

Ram's face was covered in soot. Streams of sweat ran down from his large forehead to his square jaw.

"Ram!" cried the brothers.

"Father asked to see the towers; He asked," said Ram, guilt filling his voice.

"We loaded them to show him," continued Ram. His words and memories blended into one swirling torrent.

"It went so well. I was so proud of them."

Ram paused. In his mind's eye he relived every moment.

"I didn't water them. I was going to, but we had 'til sundown. I would have watered them.

I should have watered them," Ram's voice trailed off into silence.

"They attacked without warning," he shouted, suddenly. "Father was hit. He could have died, but the Service of Light died for him; two of them!"

"Herald," shouted Shank, "signal my men to assemble near the towers. We will rain fire upon them."

"Tell the Reds to bring shields," added Falcon, "and a battering ram. We will open those gates!"

"No," came Gannon's young voice. He and Reed were running up to the tent, shouting.

"Herald," said Gannon, "Order everyone to get as far away from the walls as they can."

"Little brother," began Tulmar."

"Stop with the 'little'," shouted Gannon. "I sit at the table the same as you."

Tulmar raised his eyebrows at being spoken to in this way.

Gannon tried to think of how he could make them listen.

"Please," he begged, "Do what I say."

"Ram," he continued, "I'm sorry, but your machines are lost, pull back your men," cried Gannon in a torrent of emotion.

"Shank, please," said Gannon, "Tell the Yellows to put down their bows."

"Falcon, Falcon," cried Gannon. "Stay away from the gates, stay away from the walls."

"Gannon," replied Falcon. "What is it?"

"He has orders from Father," replied Reed.

"You spoke to Father?" shouted everyone.

"No," admitted Gannon. "He spoke to me, just after he was hit. I wasn't there. He used a signalman and he told me what to do."

"Ram," asked Falcon. "Did you see this?"

Ram frowned in concentration. He tried to remember, but his mind was all jumbled.

"Find the signalman if you don't believe him," said Reed.

"I believe him," said Falcon, "I just don't know what it means."

"I know what it means," said Gannon.

He looked full in the face of his oldest brother.

"Falcon, Father told me what to do. I've already done it. Move your men, or they will die," cried Gannon.

"I remember!" shouted Ram.

Everyone looked at Ram

"What?" they all shouted.

"Father called to one of Herald's men," said Ram. "He said to tell Gannon it was time for the Porco to meet the special passenger."

"I've already signaled *Scorpion*," said Gannon. "She'll be here any moment."

"Who?" cried Herald.

"Falcon, Herald, listen to me, please," shouted Gannon. "Pull everyone as far away from the walls as possible. Shank, please, no arrows. Tell your men to put away their arrows."

ભ ભ ભ ભ ભ

King Ahala'nn laughed as he watched the House of Hiram retreat. It was like a multi-colored wave flowing backwards after crashing weakly onto a great rock.

As he watched, something on the horizon caught his attention.

"Is that a bird?" the King asked.

He stared for a moment longer and then answered his own question.

"It can't be a bird," he told himself. "I couldn't see a bird at that distance. It's too big to be a bird, and too fast. So what is it?"

As he watched, it got bigger and closer at a mind-numbing speed. Then, it disappeared into the clouds high in the sky.

Suddenly, there came a sound, fearsome beyond measure. A horrific dragon screech came from the sky above the King.

"Shoot it," screamed King Ahala'nn. "Shoot it!"

It was a fatal mistake.

To their credit, most of the archers manning the wall stood their ground. Those who ran to safety, however, lived to tell what happened.

"Ready longbows," shouted the Captain of the archers.

The men put arrow to string and waited.

"Shoot," commanded the Captain.

The volley harmlessly struck the dragon's armored scales. It also enraged this adolescent she-dragon, which is never a good thing.

She raked the line of archers with a fiery blast from her mouth. Then, performing a perfect 180 degree aerial turn, she burned them again just for the joy of it.

"Shoot it," screamed King Ahala'nn. "Shoot it!"

So filled with himself was the King that he didn't even notice all of his men were dead.

Spying this lone royal plaything in the Upper Courtyard, the dragon closed her wings and swooped down at tremendous speed.

With a frightful cry, she snatched the King in her talons; careful not to squeeze too hard. His screams so amplified her joy that she screamed with him.

As she flew in twists and turns, the smoldering wreckage of six towers caught her attention. For a moment, it occurred to the dragon that there may be others of her kind in this land; older, wiser and stronger than she.

The dragon quickly released her plaything thus freeing her talons for dragon-battle, if needed. The King fell screaming from the sky. He landed in the Common Courtyard a few yards from General Ryguy Roces.

The general had just secured the main gate as ordered when he heard the dragon scream and saw the thing fly overhead. He watched as the King fell from the sky.

He ran to the King. Their eyes met.

"Your Majesty," said the general, gently. The King mouthed the word 'Ryguy', but died before speaking.

Perhaps I can still end this, thought General Ryguy Roces as he ran to the healing hall.

෬   ෬   ෬   ෬   ෬

"She's heading back to *Scorpion*," said Gannon as they all watched the dragon fly away.

Above them, the Upper Courtyard of the palace-fortress billowed black smoke.

"I still don't understand," confessed Ram. "You have a dragon on *Scorpion*?"

Vine, Shank and Tulmar nodded their heads. They didn't understand anything either, starting with the 'very special passenger' on *Scorpion*.

Gannon smiled sheepishly and nodded. "That's why we kept so far away from the fleet," explained Gannon. "We weren't sure she could be trusted. She gets moody."

"We built *Scorpion* with a little dragon cave in the stern," said Norrom. "Part of it is below deck and part is above."

"You knew about this?" asked Ram.

Norrom nodded. "I had to know, *Scorpion's* one of my ships, remember?" said Admiral Norrom.

"Father thought it was too risky to tell everyone," said Falcon.

"You knew, too?" cried Tulmar.

"Yes," admitted Falcon. "Some Reds guarded her."

"It was a hard secret to keep," said Reed.

"You knew?" asked Vine.

"I always keep secrets," explained Reed. "The Greens are full of secrets. That's what we do."

"Anybody else?" asked Tulmar.

Herald chortled uncomfortably; "Only me," he said, "and two of my signalmen."

"Of course," said Tulmar, sarcastically.

"We had to signal between the ships," explained Herald.

"And the crew of *Scorpion*," added Gannon.

"Is that all?" asked Ram, dumfounded.

Quasar and Nemo kept very quiet.

"Well, Father, of course," said Norrom.

"Of course," said Ram.

"And the crew of *Vengeance*, too," added Norrom.

"That's great," said Shank. "That's just great! Are we the only ones who didn't know?"

"It really is great!" exclaimed Gannon, hoping to change the subject. "Just look what she did to King Ahala'nn and the archers who shot Father."

Ram, Vine, Shank and Tulmar had to admit that the dragon had really helped, today.

"And she lives on *Scorpion*?" asked Ram.

"She really likes *Scorpion*," said Gannon. "Sometimes she sits on the mast, but she's getting a little heavy for that, now." Gannon smiled. "She thinks of *Scorpion* as her home."

"How do you know what she thinks?" asked Shank.

"I can talk to her," said Gannon.

"You speak dragon?" shouted Shank and Tulmar at the same time.

Gannon shook his head. "No," he said. *Don't be ridiculous*, he wanted to say. Instead he added, "But, I do speak elfin and so does she."

"I'm afraid to ask," began Shank, "but how did she learn elfin?"

"The elves taught her, of course," answered Gannon. *How else would someone learn elfin?* he thought. But he held his tongue.

"Can we go inside the Command Tent?" asked Quasar. "This is going to get complicated."

All eyes turned toward Quasar. He had a funny little smile on his face. Nemo stood next to him, blushing.

"You don't think this is complicated already, Dragon-Slayer?" asked Shank. The corners of his mouth turned up, just a little.

"It gets better," answered Nemo with a chuckle.

Falcon and his brothers gave orders for their men to take the wounded to the healing tents. Gannon's men went about the dismal job of gathering the dead.

Reed posted guards all around the palace-fortress and sentries around the borders of the camp. Shank added archers to watch the fortress walls.

Vine sent orders for his men to begin serving dinner to the camp and to bring food to the Command Tent. A few minutes later, platters heaped with roasted chicken, bowls of steaming hot potatoes, baskets of bread, sweet cakes and large teapots were brought to the tent.

As each of the brothers finished their tasks, they made their way to the Command Tent. Ram was the last to arrive.

"I've just come from the healing tents, he announced upon entering.

"I have good news. There are a lot less dead than we imagined; more wounded, but less dead. The healers believe most will live."

"What about Father?" asked Falcon.

A cloud passed over Ram's face.

"Father was wounded deeply by the arrow," he said sadly. "The point broke off within him."

Ram looked at each of his brothers, trying to see if they blamed him. They did not.

"The healers had to dig the point out and he bled too much," said Ram, simply. "He is resting now."

Ram forced a smile. "He'll be fine," he assured them and himself. "He is strong and stubborn."

"Like you," said Tulmar, good-naturedly.

"Like me," replied Ram.

He smiled for the first time since the Lord Hiram was shot.

Ram took his place at the table.

"Just to make sure I understand," he began, "You have a dragon on *Scorpion* that speaks to you in elfin and thinks the ship is her home. Is that right?"

"That pretty much sums it up," said Gannon, lightly.

"I'm going to need a little more," said Ram.

"I think we all are," said Tulmar with just a smudge of a smile.

Quasar paced around the tent as he began to explain about the dragon.

"This goes all the way back to the Battle of Three Rivers in Draamor," said Quasar.

"Can we get the short version," asked Ram. "I'm hungry."

"You'd better eat while I talk," replied Quasar.

"Well, in that case," said Falcon.

He stood, and looking much like his father, closed his eyes and lifting an arm straight up, offered a prayer of thanks. When he was finished, food was passed around the table.

Sitting, Falcon nodded to Quasar and said, "If you please, Dragon-Slayer."

Everyone laughed.

"Our dragon is the hatchling of the one that helped us win the Battle of Three Rivers," said Quasar.

"What?" exclaimed everyone at the table.

Some of them talked with their mouths full of food, but we can excuse them. It's not every day you learn you have a dragon.

"You remember her," Quasar exclaimed. "She died killing the dragons that were fighting us in the Battle of Three Rivers."

"How could we forget," said Norrom. "She saved us. Without her we would have lost. Please pass me some tea," he asked Vine.

"Thanks."

"Before she helped us," said Quasar, "Nemo and I killed all the eggs in her lair except one. That one is our dragon, today."

"How can that be?" exclaimed Tulmar. "How could she survive? Who raised her?" he asked. "Is there any more bread?"

"We made a deal with her mother," said Nemo, simply. "She kept her word and so did we."

"When the old dragon died," explained Quasar, "the elves reclaimed their mountain and all the gold in her lair. Most of it was stolen from them, anyway. The egg was with the gold."

"Why didn't the elves kill the egg when they had the chance?" asked Ram, between bites of roasted chicken.

"It took the elves weeks and weeks to cart all the gold back to The Kingdom of Light," said Quasar.

"Glendeux, King of the Elves; the People of Light ordered them to leave the egg alone," added Nemo.

"It was part of the deal," added Quasar.

"Finally," continued Nemo, "when the lair was all but empty, the egg began to move and crack."

"The King himself was in the cave when the hatchling fought her way out of the shell," said Quasar.

"The King was the first thing she saw when she opened her eyes for the very first time," said Nemo. "She thinks of the King as her mother. He carried her all the way to the Kingdom of Light, himself. By the time they got there, they had bonded."

"That's incredible," said Reed. "Who would believe the King of the elves raised a dragon? Does anyone want half of this potato?

"Some of the elves opposed the King," said Quasar; "Especially those who had lost family fighting her mother," added Nemo.

"I'll take half, if nobody else wants it," said Ram.

"You already have a whole potato on your plate," said Reed.

"So," replied Ram. "I said, 'if nobody else wants it' and nobody else wants it."

Reed shrugged his shoulders and passed the potato to Ram.

"In the end," continued Quasar," King Glendeux won them all over. The People of Light raised the dragon in their forest."

"That is the most astounding thing I have ever heard," said Falcon. "Do you know the history of elves and dragons?" he asked. "It's astonishing!"

"It is amazing to think a dragon actually lived with elves!" exclaimed Norrom.

"She thinks she's an elf," said Nemo, quietly. "Pass me a sweet cake, please."

"What?" everyone cried.

"A sweet cake," said Nemo, a little surprised. "I only had one."

"You had two," corrected Quasar.

Nemo glared at him. "Ok, two. May I have another sweet cake?"

Sweet cakes were Nemo's favorite food in the whole world.

Vine passed him not one but two more sweet cakes.

"Did you say the dragon thinks she's an elf?" asked Vine.

"You should see her," said Nemo in between bites of sweet cake. "It's really funny."

"But that's where the problems started," said Quasar. "When she was little, it was cute. Then she started growing up."

"She's a juvenile now," said Nemo. It's not cute anymore. She has mood swings," he said, laughing a little.

"The elves raised her vegetarian," said Nemo, "but one day she discovered she likes meat. She really likes meat; she keeps raiding sheep and cattle ranches."

"The day she learned she could breathe fire, she burned up part of the elfin forest," said Quasar. "That was the last straw."

"Anyway, that's when the King contacted Father and asked for help," said Falcon.

"We were going to bring her to an island with plenty of wild animals and not many people, but now," said Falcon with a big smile, "I think I have a better idea."

Suddenly, the tent flap opened and a Green rushed in. It was the very same man who had rushed in twice before.

"I'm sorry to interrupt, you Sirs," said the man, "but there is something you all should see."

"What is it?" asked Lord Reed.

"The fortress gates have opened and the general who was here before is coming," said the man. "We think he is carrying a body."

෪ ෪ ෪ ෪ ෪

As General Ryguy Roces slowly walked down from the main gate, he could see a large group gathering on the main road.

The nine sons of the House of Hiram stood in line in the order of their birth. Around them was the Service of Light, forming a human circle of protection. Quasar and Nemo stood quietly off to one side.

What the general could not see were the Reds, Greens and Yellows deployed behind nearby rocks and bushes and sand dunes.

General Ryguy Roces was dressed in his finest uniform. He was leading his horse on which were laid two bodies.

"I am unarmed," he shouted as he approached the fearsome guards dressed all in white.

One of them stopped him and searched him, the bodies and the horse. When satisfied, the guard brought the general to Lord Falcon.

Falcon looked at the general without blinking and remained silent. Tension grew. Even the horse seemed on edge with ears back, flicking his tail.

"It is almost sundown," said the general, finally. "I have come to keep my word."

"We tried to avoid bloodshed, General," said Falcon, "yet many, today, have bled."

"Lord Falcon," said General Ryguy Roces, humbly. "Please believe me. I tried everything I could to stop them."

"Look there," said the general, pointing to the fortress. "The gates are open. I commanded them to remain open for you. I ordered the men to disarm. There are no more archers on the walls. Those who harmed you are dead."

"I see," said Falcon.

"You wanted proof that Prince Rhala'nn has seen justice. Lord Falcon, I bring you his body. As I already told you, he was killed by his own father, King Ahala'nn. I bring the King's body as well, killed by your fire-breather."

The general handed the reins of his horse to Lord Falcon. Falcon in turn passed them to one of the Service of Light. The horse was led to the side.

"General Ryguy Roces," began Falcon. "You have forgotten the first thing, the main thing, and the foremost thing," said Falcon. His voice and eyes were hard.

"Where are our wives, General," asked Falcon?

General Ryguy Roces took a deep breath and tried to form his words. He cleared his throat and said, "Most of the Favored Ones," he stopped and corrected himself. "Most of the kidnapped women are in the fortress. We know where they are. They are as well as can be expected."

The general tried to think of how to tell this man that his wife was still missing.

Just tell him the truth, thought Ryguy.

"Lord Falcon," began the general. "I wish with all my being that I could give you a better answer about Lady Cilantra and her friend Brittany. If I knew where they were I would bring them to you. The truth is, sir, I do not know where they are."

General Ryguy Roces braced himself for Falcon's wrath. He did not know if he would be killed outright or have to pay with pain. He was unprepared for what happened next.

Falcon looked intently at the man for what seemed like hours, and then smiled graciously.

"I'm glad to see, General, that you are a man whom I can trust."

Falcon motioned with his hand. The Service of Light parted and two beautiful women walked serenely toward the general. One had hair like ebony and the other hair like gold.

They stopped at Falcon's side and were joined by a young man.

"General Ryguy Roces, said the Lord Falcon. "I present to you my wife, Lady Cilantra, her friend Brittany and Brittany's husband, Quasar the Dragon-Slayer.

General Ryguy Roces stood speechless. He blinked and tried to speak several times, before finally saying, "I'm so glad you found them."

"As are we, General," said Falcon. "You should know General, that the words just spoken in truth saved your life and your country."

"Thank, you," was all the general could think to say.

The Service of Light respectfully lowered the two bodies from the general's horse onto the ground.

Falcon escorted Cilantra toward the bodies. Quasar followed with Brittany. The women looked briefly at the bodies.

Without hesitation Cilantra said, "I never saw the King, and I only saw the Prince once, briefly in passing. But, that is the Prince. I'm sure."

Brittany nodded. "Our kidnapper is dead, she said quietly." Brittany turned and hid her face, safe in Quasar's arms.

"General Ryguy Roces," said Falcon. "We have much to discuss. Will you break bread with me and my brothers and hear the terms of your surrender?"

"We just ate," whispered Ram.

"That never stopped you before," replied Vine, with a smile.

"It would be an honor," said the general. "And thank you for my life."

"You may not wish to thank me once you hear what I have to say," said Falcon, coolly.

A shiver ran down the general's back. Cilantra glanced at her husband. Nemo and Quasar stared at Falcon. Brittany covered her mouth with her hand.

"Your king is dead," explained Falcon, "and so is his only heir." Falcon smiled a little and then said, "It seems to me that you, General, may end up being the next ruler of the precious sands of Saalespor."

Cilantra and Brittany smiled, Quasar nodded his head and Nemo laughed. The general just stood and blinked, saying nothing.

C3　C 3　C 3　C 3　C 3

The oil lamps in the Command Tent hissed and popped. It was very late, but all that needed to be said was finally said.

"So we are agreed?" asked Falcon.

"Yes," said General Ryguy Roces. "The fortress is yours. The gates are already open," he said. "And my men are already disarmed."

"If there are no problems, General," said Falcon, "their weapons may be returned to them once we leave. For now, everyone must stay unarmed and indoors."

"You're right, of course," said the general. "The sight of gold can make good men do foolish things."

"My men will bring wagons into the fortress," said Norrom. "Half of King Ahala'nn's treasury will be brought to our ships as payment for the blood and treasure we have spent."

"I understand," said General Ryguy Roces.

"Your navy must return to the slave market and buy the freedom of every slave they sold. None of that blood money will come to Saalespor."

"It will be done," said the general. "I will send a ship to find them tomorrow," he promised solemnly.

"Today," said Falcon.

"Excuse me?" said the general.

"We have talked all night," explained Falcon. "It is sunrise."

"I will send a ship today," agreed the general. He risked a small smile.

"The other half of King Ahala'nn's gold will be brought to the caves," said Norrom. Saalespor is now our dragon's new home."

"Forgive me," said the general. "I don't understand that part," he said humbly. "You are leaving half of King Ahala'nn's gold behind?"

"We are leaving the dragon behind," answered Gannon. "She will live in the cave that Brock found."

"Dragons love gold," explained Falcon. "We hope the gold in the cave will convince her to make Saalespor her new home."

"I see," said the general, slowly. "What are we supposed to do with her?" he asked.

"Keep her happy," said Reed with a smile.

"Remember, she thinks she is an elf," added Gannon. "Elves love justice and goodness and honor and light," said Gannon. "The more your people develop these traits the happier she will be."

"So, she is to be our tutor?" asked the general."

"Perhaps," said Falcon. "I would think of her as more like your Sheriff," he said with a sparkle in his eye.

"I see," said the general, cautiously.

"There is one more matter," said Cilantra. "The Favored Ones, so called," she sighed. "The kidnapped ones must be returned home."

Everyone nodded, but the general.

"Forgive me," he began, "but some don't want to leave. They like their new life here better than their old life."

"Those who wish to stay, of course may stay," said Falcon; "but not as Favored Ones. They must be free to live and work as anyone else." Falcon did not smile when he said this.

"The 'work' part might change their minds," said Brittany. "With freedom comes responsibility. It is a hard lesson for some."

The tent became quiet.

"They must be made to understand," said Cilantra, "that if they stay they will not live in the palace, having servants and cooks and silk clothes."

"Their lives will be what they make of them," added Brittany, "through honest hard work."

"There is just one more thing, said Norrom. "Those who want to go home should be returned home as quickly as possible. Their families are still grieving," he explained.

Everyone agreed.

"They should sail," continued Norrom, "aboard *The Black Claw* tomorrow or the next day at the latest."

"No!" cried Cilantra. "No!"

"I would rather die than set foot on that ship again," cried Brittany.

"Hear me, please," implored Narrom. "She will no longer be *The Black Claw*," he promised. "She is a sound ship, and fast. We should use her."

He looked at Brittany and Cilantra and smiled reassuringly.

"She will be cleansed and reborn. The chains will be removed. New sleeping quarters will be arranged. You will not recognize her. I guarantee it," said Norrom.

Falcon and Quasar wrapped their wives in strong loving arms.

"I will ask Brock to captain her," said Norrom, after a few moments of silence. He looked compassionately at Cilantra and Brittany.

"Brock tried to rescue you," he said gently. "He lost his own ship, *Emeraldsea* in this nightmare. It is only right that we give him a new one."

Cilantra looked at Falcon and then at Norrom. It made sense, but it was still hard to hear. She nodded her head, slightly.

Brittany looked up from Quasar's arms and wiped away her tears.

"Will she have a new name," asked Brittany, meekly.

"Yes," smiled Norrom. "You and Cilantra can name her," declared Norrom.

Suddenly, the tent flap opened and the inside of the tent was set ablaze with bright morning sunlight.

"Father!" cried Ram.

The Lord Hiram stood in the brightness of a new day; strong and whole.

"What are you all doing in here?" he asked, smiling broadly. "We have work to do," he said smiling. "It's sunrise!"

14663924R00194

Made in the USA
San Bernardino, CA
01 September 2014